The Sacrifices of One Woman

By
Linnette James-Sow

Linnette James-Sow

Strategic Book Group

Strategic Book Group
P.O. Box 333
Durham, Ct. 06422
www.StrategicBookClub.com

ISBN: 978-1-61204-031-8

Book Design: Prepress-Solutions.com

Introduction

It is difficult to remain who you are after falling in love since, more often than not, you are expected to alter and adjust your lifestyle in order to accommodate the other person's needs. I believe they call it compromising; however, through these life-changing moments, people can sometimes lose themselves, trying to please the other person more than they feel the need to please themselves. In doing so, they've forgotten who they are.

The need to be able to make provision for our kids and our families has sometimes resulted in us making decisions about marriages and relationships that can be detrimental to the emotional, mental, and psychosocial well-being of ourselves and our families. Some women stay in relationships that are far from fulfilling because, in their eyes, they're trying to do their best for their families; or they stay because they're just too frightened to be alone.

The reality is you'll never really understand someone else's situation until you are in that situation yourself. It's so easy to say, "It could never happen to me." But the heart is a very powerful organ of the body. It functions in ways that, even as its owner, you have no control of.

Sometimes we just can't help whom we fall in love with or how we react to love when it happens. However, it takes a strong individual to make a relationship work, and it takes an even stronger individual to walk away from a relationship that's destructive. For most of us women, we do the best we know how with the situation at the time. That decision may not have been the best choice, but we may have made those decisions as our means of survival.

* * *

This is a story about one woman and her journey through her unhappy marriage. In order to make financial provisions for her children, she endured suffering as a married woman.

Cheryl was a confident and outgoing woman who had never sought love and reassurance outside of herself. But after years of being married to a powerful man who sought to exert his power through the use of inducing fear, she gradually lost herself and became the woman her husband wanted her to be.

Table of Contents

Chapter 1

    Having to raise two children on her own wasn't a predicament that Cheryl thought she would ever have to experience, since she herself was raised in a two-parent family and no one in her own circle of friends was a single mom. Cheryl never imagined that her life could have changed so drastically, from once being a happily married woman, with a husband who adored her and their children, to being a single mom who had to worry about the financial well-being of herself and her children. Cheryl walked out of her marriage two years ago. It was the hardest decision she had ever made in her life. The separation was, however, short-lived, as she returned home shortly afterward.

    Terry and Cheryl got married after finishing university. She had studied to become a pharmacist, and he, a surgeon. They didn't really date each other openly prior to getting married, since Cheryl's background didn't permit this. Cheryl was from a deeply religious household; her dad was a Baptist minister, and her mom was a housewife. Having a relationship outside of marriage was deeply frowned upon by Cheryl's parents, as it was considered to be disobeying the teaching of the Bible, as the Bible forbid a sexual relationship outside of marriage, and is thus written as one of the Ten Commandments. Cheryl's mom was a an extremely hard working woman, and had held many jobs, from working in nursing homes to lifting boxes in warehouses and factories, in order to finance her education at university prior to meeting and marrying Cheryl's dad—and her education had helped her garnered a flourishing teaching career. Cheryl's mother had taught children between the ages of nine and eleven at one of the local schools before she met and married Cheryl's dad.

Cheryl's dad had a limited education; he had never been to university and left school with only two general certificate secondary education (GCSEs) before commencing Bible study at a local college, whilst working as a bus driver.

At her dad's request, her mom gave up her job as a teacher after the birth of their first child, Cheryl's sister. Her father was an old-fashioned man who believed that a woman's place was at home, taking care of her family.

After Cheryl's mom gave up her job as a teacher, she focused on raising Trinny, Cheryl's sister, and giving her husband the support he needed in order to make his ministerial post flourish. Her mother was the brain behind her dad, helping him with his assignments that he brought home from college. She also played the role of the dutiful wife and always had dinner on the table when he returned from work. Since they were living on only one income, he often worked long hours to make ends meet at home.

Cheryl's dad continued to drive buses during his early ministerial post, since the church that he was assigned to back in 1974, was a small church, and he didn't received much from the "tithe and offering" that was collected each Sunday. It wasn't until after Cheryl's birth, a year later, that her dad was assigned to a much bigger church, one with a congregation of two thousand people. This meant that they had to move, since this church was seventy miles away from where they were living, and the long drive back and forth, with two babies in tow, would make commuting overwhelming.

The relationship between Cheryl's mom and dad seemed perfect: her dad was the head of the house, and although her mom sacrificed her career for him, she didn't seem to have any regrets. She relished being his wife and cherished being at home with her kids, where she had the opportunity to see, firsthand, every milestone in their lives. *This is every mom's dream,* Cheryl's mom thought. Cheryl's mom never complained, and she seemed to be happy in choosing to stand by her man, as opposed to pursuing a career for herself. Cheryl had memories of how proud her mom became at the mention of her husband's name or ministry.

They were a well-respected family in the little town where they lived, and to be the wife and kids of a pastor was an honour. It was at her dad's church that Cheryl was to meet her future husband, Terry. Terry's parents weren't Christians, but they would occasionally visit Dad's church, especially for special occasions, such as Christmas services. Cheryl ran into Terry in the corridors of the church at the end of Sunday services, but she never gave him a second glance. There wasn't anything remarkable about Terry; he was stocky and had a protruding belly that made him look as if he were at least four months pregnant. He had a small and pointy nose that slightly leaned to the left side of his face—a boxer's nose, she called it.

It wasn't until Cheryl started university, in 1993, that she became interested in him. By this time, Terry had biceps that were so large they were visible through his shirts, and his stomach could rival a gladiator's.

Terry was a man of the world. He was older than Cheryl by only five years, but he seemed to have a wealth of worldly experience. He had had several girlfriends, had a social life that involved visiting nightclubs on the weekends, and was a heavy weekend-drinker.

Cheryl on the other hand, who had lived a sheltered life, had never had a serious relationship with a man and had no idea what the inside of a nightclub looked liked. She wasn't a smoker either, and her only encounter with alcohol was so horrible, that it put her off alcohol for the rest of her life. One winter, just after Cheryl's twenty-first birthday, her cousin returned from a visit to the Caribbean, she brought home some Caribbean rum.

As Cheryl sat and watched her make a cocktail of Caribbean rum and Coke, she developed an appetite for the cocktail herself when her cousin would take a sip of the concoction and then close her eyes and make small sounds of pleasure. Cheryl could only imagine that whatever sensation this woman was feeling, it was to die for, and she wanted to experience this herself.

"You dunna wat yu missing," said the cousin, with a strong Jamaican accent, letting her tongue linger over her lips.

Cheryl thought that this was the closest she was ever going to get to an orgasm, being a virgin, so she decided to give into her cousin's temptation. Cheryl took a mouthful of the drink and swallowed it, and what came next was sheer horror. As the drink went past her tongue and made its way down her throat, she felt like it was taking out pieces of her oesophagus along with it, chunk by chunk. If Cheryl hadn't trusted her cousin, she would have and could have easily accused her of "lacing her drink with acid," because it certainly felt as though she had swallowed battery acid, not a cocktail of Coca-Cola and Caribbean rum. After that experience, Cheryl never tried any form of alcohol again.

Cheryl and Terry started dating in 1995, after he met her in the Birmingham central library, which she frequently visited because she found it to have more resources than her local library. Her best friend, Angel, also lived in Birmingham, and on Cheryl's weekend visits, they'd both visit the library before embarking on their shopping spree.

Cheryl was a great lover of clothes, although she had little money to spend on them, being a student. But she had the skills to co-ordinate outfits so that not only did she look stylish, but she also made it difficult for observers to realize that she had worn them before. She loved shoes with heels and would rarely be seen out not wearing a pair, and her feet had enough corns and bunions to show the history.

Cheryl and Angel would travel from county to county, visiting the high streets, looking for bargains at the stores. Cheryl had a diverse wardrobe, but did make an effort to avoid anything that was above her knees, too low cut, or too tight, because she considered this look to be cheap and tarty.

Angel, on the other hand, relished the attention she received from both men and women when she wore such clothing and considered Cheryl's dress sense to be old-fashioned, since she never wore any outfits that displayed her legs or breasts.

Angel was of dual heritage and had tightly curled brown hair with streaks of blond, all of which were natural. She was of average height, but she was cursed with rather short, stumpy legs, which robbed her of at least two inches in appearance. However, what she lacked in height, she sure made up for in beauty. She had a light brown complexion and had the most beautiful eyes that God had ever created for any human being. Her eyes were as bright as the sun on a very hot day, and they were so large it would be impossible to miss her in the dark, even in the pitch black. She had a little plump nose that just fitted neatly in the centre of her face. She had an arresting presence, and all heads turned to look at her when she walked in a room. Sometimes it was difficult to tell whether they were staring because of her beauty or because she looked tarty, but nonetheless, she was always the centre of attention.

Angel was one of the few people who knew of Cheryl and Terry's secret liaison, and so was well informed of their first date. She was flabbergasted when told by Cheryl where Terry would be taking her for their first date, as she was aware that only the very affluent dined at such restaurants.

For their first date, Terry took Cheryl out for an Indian meal at one of Birmingham's plushest restaurants. Terry was a regular visitor of the Wood Bridge Road area in Birmingham, known for its Indian cuisine and vast number of Asian restaurants, which cooked appetizing meals that left a lingering taste in the mouth long after it was eaten. His favourite restaurant in the area was Meroush. He liked the restaurant, because it was unique in its preparation of its food, and its scenery was breathtaking. It stood out from all the other restaurants that he had visited over the years, both in England and across the globe, in that there were no tables and chairs in it. Diners had to dine on exquisite antiques rugs. It was a restaurant with a difference.

The atmosphere in Meroush was rather romantic, with its rugs with red and white roses laid out on the floor. The lights were dimmed so that they were just bright enough for diners to be able to see their meals. The walls were covered with mirrors that were decorated with gold frames, and the gas fireplace glowed in the semi-dark room. A selection of Asian music played in the background. Although Cheryl wasn't able to understand the lyrics of the songs, she could feel the passion of the tunes.

When she looked at Terry, sitting opposite her, she knew she was destined to marry this man. Her stomach made several gymnastic moves that night while she experienced an array of emotions that she had never encountered before.

Terry was excited about the flavours on his plate and often demanded that Cheryl try a taste of his dishes, feeding her with his bare hands. To her, this was not only a romantic gesture, but it also highlighted Terry's caring side, demonstrating that it was important to him that his date was having as much pleasure as he was on their night out.

Cheryl ordered chocolate cake buried in ice cream for pudding, but Terry refused to have any pudding.

'I'm not a pudding man,' he tried to explain. 'Watching my figure,' he added, teasing.

Cheryl found this rather amusing, and she reflected on the earlier days, when she would go by him in church without giving him a second look. Back then, he had what could easily be described as a beer belly. His shirts always looked like they were two sizes too small, and his trousers hung below his belly, so low that if it hadn't been for his underpants, you would have gotten a flash of his pubic hair. He looked older than his years then. You could have easily mistaken him for his dad's older brother. *Perhaps he fears returning back to that old self,* Cheryl silently mused.

As she sat eating her dessert, her mouth occasionally got messy from the ice cream. Terry leaned across the rug and used his fingers to clean her mouth, then proceeded to stick his fingers in his own mouth and lick them. Cheryl wasn't entirely sure how to respond to this gesture and just giggled with embarrassment at his behaviour.

'Your lips are the most tender I've ever felt,' he expressed after he wiped her mouth for the second time.

He then placed his finger on her lips and let his thumb slide across her mouth. Cheryl felt a tingling sensation ran down the back of her neck. She opened her mouth, almost spontaneously, to allow his fingers in her mouth. Her clitoris gave a beat, and she closed her eyes. She lost herself for a moment when he grasped her face with his other hand. She was about to let out a sound of pleasure when she suddenly remembered her cousin's expression on that night she was drinking rum and Coke. She blushed with embarrassment, and pulled her head back so that his fingers would fall free from her mouth.

He was bemused by the sudden change in her behaviour. 'Have I gone too far?' he asked with a worried expression.

'No, no,' she replied, trying to disguise her humiliation. The truth was, Cheryl enjoyed and liked every moment of his fingers exploring her lips, mouth, and face, so much that it brought her close to an orgasm. This she found terribly embarrassing, as it was only their first date. And she had never heard of anyone achieving an orgasm by licking someone's fingers.

They ended the night by going to a nightclub, where she spent the night drinking orange juice, he nursed Jack Daniels, and both danced the night away to a mixture of reggae, hip hop, and ballads.

Terry was a great dancer and was packed with rhythm. He could dance to any tune and made it looked so easy, gliding from one genre of music to the other. He would do the skank when it came to reggae and easily made the transition to break dance when the DJ played hip hop. When it was time for the ballads, he scooped Cheryl in his arms and pulled her in close to him.

While mirroring his foot movements, her eyes locked with his. He moved in closer to her, and by then, they were inhaling each other's breath. He rubbed his nose against hers, and she responded by mimicking his actions. He held her tightly around the waist and bent forward to place his head on her shoulders. She placed her face against his chest and could feel the heat that was generated from under his shirt. He was hot and sticky from all the dancing he had done. Under all that heat and sweat came a repulsive smell that made Cheryl hold her breath for most of their close contact. It turned out to be his aftershave.

'I wish I could keep you this close to me,' he whispered in her ear.

'This feels good,' she replied, trying not to inhale the odour of his aftershave. She wished she could tell him how repulsive it was, but she held back, thinking it would make her seem rude, and she didn't want him to have a negative impression about her on their first date. So she kept this a secret. Besides, Cheryl had never had this much fun in her twenty-plus years of life. She felt particularly free and was able to let her hair down, and since she was forty-four miles away from home, she knew it was unlikely that she would bump into anyone from her dad's church.

After that first date, Cheryl knew that he was the one.

Chapter 2

They were from different backgrounds. Cheryl had a humble, working class background, whilst Terry had a more affluent and extravagant upbringing. His parents had emigrated from Syria in the 1960s. His dad was a director of a chain of supermarkets, and his mom was a psychiatrist. Terry was the youngest of three brothers, and on the occasional Sundays when he and his family would go to Cheryl's church, they turned up in a Jaguar that was driven by his dad, or a Range Rover that was driven by his mom.

Money never seemed to be an issue in Terry's household, and he was always decked out in the latest designs. (Like Cheryl, he loved his fashion, but unlike her, he had the money to spend on the most exquisite outfits.) But these suits didn't make him stand out from the crowd because, back then, he looked unkempt due to his physique.

Over the next few months, they had several more dates, and had it not been for Terry's aftershave, he would have been flawless on each occasion. Cheryl now felt confident being with him, and although they had been together for only seven months, she felt that she could be open with him, and he, with her.

One night, as they danced away to Gladys Knight singing 'Georgia,' she buried her face under his arm and attempted to breathe through her mouth. Her efforts proved to be unsuccessful; she became dizzy from trying to hold her breath for such long periods.

'I don't need to worry about being pestered by insects when I'm with you,' Cheryl jokingly told Terry.

'Why?' he asked, perplexed.

'Your aftershave …'

'What about it?' he asked curiously.

'It smells like insect spray,' she retorted.

'You cheeky madam! This cost me a fortune,' he said indignantly.

'They saw you coming,' she fired back, referring to the manufacturer of the aftershave.

They laughed that evening until Cheryl wet her pants. They were captivated by each other's presence. There was never a dull moment when they were together, and it was heart-wrenchingly painful when they had to be apart.

They kept their relationship hidden from Cheryl's parents for the next year, since having a relationship outside of marriage would have been detrimental to her dad's career. He would have lost the respect of the church because his daughter would be considered to be a fornicator, whether she had done the deed or not.

For the past year of their relationship, Cheryl and Terry had never been intimate with each other, other than kissing and groping. She could remember the first time that he kissed her. They had just been to see the film *The Body Guard*. When Terry opened his car door to usher her in, he put his arm around her tiny waist and kissed her on her nose. As they gazed into each other's eyes, Terry locked his lips with hers and insinuated his tongue into her mouth. Cheryl was unsure what to do with his tongue, since she'd never had anyone's tongue in her mouth before. So she opened her mouth as wide as she possibly could, leaned into him, and let his tongue move around her mouth.

Terry could tell by her response that she was inexperienced. She wasn't like the other girls whom he'd been out with before. His last girlfriend had a PhD in love-making and had introduced him to positions that he didn't know existed. But he viewed these past relationships as only a bit of fun, since he was not ready to settle down, nor did he have any interest in a woman who could create positions in the bedroom that made her look like a gymnast; he saw these women as 'used up,' since they must have already been with several men.

Terry's parents loved Cheryl because they perceived her to be innocent and believed that her being with Terry would have a positive influence on him. In the second year of their relationship, Terry discussed with Cheryl the possibility of disclosing their relationship to her parents, since he intended to make her his wife.

Cheryl was elated by this because her dream was about to come true. She knew, from their first date, that he would be hers one day. For the introduction, Cheryl thought that it would be best if she invited her parents out for a meal because her dad was unlikely to show his anger in public if he disapproved of Terry.

That night, Terry chose his outfit tentatively. He wanted to make a good impression on Mr. and Mrs. Bradley and was eager for them to approve of him, but he was nervous. Here he was, about to ask for the hand of the woman whom he totally adored—her hand in marriage from a man who was portrayed as being as holy as Christ. *What if he gets a revelation about my past just by looking at me?* Terry began to question himself. *What if he starts to rebuke me and asks the Holy Spirit to cast out my demons, like I've seen him done in church?*

This was the very man whom he had witnessed display incredible power one Sunday afternoon back in the summer of 88, when he was just a teenager. A young man had walked into the church and had sat in the second row of seats back from the altar. What transpired then was unbelievable to Terry and his family—they had never visited any other denomination outside of Catholicism and had never seen anything of its kind before. A short and stocky woman, who must have been in her mid-fifties, dressed in a grey suit and matching hat, stood up and started to shout out in what appeared to be a foreign tongue. (Terry later learnt that this was called 'speaking in tongues.') This occurred when the Holy Spirit anointed someone and manifested Himself through the use of language that is never understood. The woman went over to a young man and started to jump around him; she was soon joined by Cheryl's dad.

'I cast you out!' he proclaimed. 'Every demonic force, I compel you to leave this young man's body!' He pointed his hand at the man, as if to cast a spell, and when he did, the man fell to the floor, motionless, with froth coming from his mouth.

Terry started to have flashbacks about the many women he had fornicated with, as he made his preparation to meet his in-laws. There was one woman in particular whom he couldn't erase from his mind. She was the wife of Terry's elder brother, narcissistic friend, Mark. Paula was her name. She was a pretty blond who stood at 5 feet 2 inches; she had piercing blue eyes and the warmest smile.

Terry despised Mark, an arrogant man who showed no respect for anyone, not even his wife. And he often felt sorry for Paula because she looked like a woman who had the world on her head when she wasn't smiling. Mark had never shown any warmth toward her; as far as Terry could gather, and she was often left at home with their six-month-old baby, whilst he went out with other women on the weekends.

Terry had met Paula through Markus, who had taken him to the couple's house after his son was born 'to wet the head.' Terry was struck by her beauty and got an instant erection when she took her breast out to feed her then five-day-old son. The second time he saw Paula was outside of a supermarket, after he saw her struggling to look after a screaming baby and trying to load a mountain of groceries into her car. She was close to tears when Terry approached her and offered to help. He could tell by her reaction that she welcomed his help and was very appreciative of it.

'He's just filled his nappy and must be feeling uncomfortable,' she said with frustration.

Terry saw this as a means to get closer to Paula. 'Is Mark at home to help you?' he asked, knowing what the answer would be.

'No,' Paula replied.

'I'll follow you home and give you a hand unpacking,' he stated.

Paula welcomed this idea and changed little Timmy's nappy before she set off.

When they arrived at Paula's home, Terry pulled in the drive, behind Paula's car. He hastily jumped out of his car, rushed over to hers, and grabbed a few shopping bags before she could step out of her car. As she exited the car, Terry told her to concentrate on little Timmy whilst he unloaded the car. Paula was far less stressed by now and couldn't be more thankful for Terry's help. She was able to feed and put Timmy to bed whilst Terry unpacked the groceries from the car.

Paula couldn't help but think of how different it would be if Mark were around to help her more with both the housework and attending to Timmy. As she stood watching Terry in her kitchen, she felt herself becoming instantly attracted to him. This was a woman with a six-month-old baby who was married to a man who was hardly ever there for them. Her circle of friends often referred to him as 'a slimy eel,' since they were all aware of his infidelity. He was rarely home and spent much of his time chasing anything in a skirt, so it didn't take much for her to feel loved by another man.

Kneeling, Terry unpacked the groceries into the lower cupboards. Unaware that Paula was standing so close to him, he bumped into her when he stood up. He opened his mouth to apologize, but when his eyes met with hers, he could see that she secretly longed for him.

Before he could utter a word, their lips met. Paula started panting heavily; she had kissed a few men before marrying Mark, but none had kissed her with such passion as this. She lifted her neck and allowed her head to fall back, an invitation for Terry to take things further. He ran his lips down her neck and buried his face between her breasts, letting his tongue taste her skin as he went along. He pulled her bra under her breast, and two humongous breasts fell out. They were rounded and firm, and if it hadn't been for the stretch marks that were visible on them, he wouldn't have known that Paula had just had a baby, as her stomach was flat and toned, giving no indication that she was pregnant just six months ago. He grabbed hold of them both, and they felt different from the other women's breasts that he had caressed in the past. They felt hard and particularly firm. As he continued to grope Paula's breasts, he could feel a tiny scar under one of them. He immediately concluded that her breasts were surgically enhanced, but this was, by no means, a turn-off for him.

He tried to put both nipples in his mouth at once, but they were not supple and flexible and couldn't be manipulated like he wished. Paula had unzipped him by now and was fondling his scrotum. He lifted her onto the kitchen counter, and as he placed his face against her pubic hair, a key could be heard turning in the front door.

'Paula!' A voice screamed from the front door.

'Oh my God, it's Mark!' she whispered.

She jumped from the counter, straightening her clothes. Terry pulled up his trousers, which were lying around his ankles, and quickly pulled his zipper up, and then wet his hand with saliva and quickly brushed back his hair.

'In here!' she replied.

Mark headed for the kitchen, oblivious to what had just taken place.

'Hey, Terry! What brought you here?'

'He found me struggling at the supermarket and offered to give a hand,' Paula replied.

A look of embarrassment came over Mark's face because he knew that if he suggested that Paula do the shopping during the weekend, when he was off from work, then he could have helped and she wouldn't have struggled. He felt his inadequacy as a husband had been exposed.

'Thank you,' he said shyly.

The affair went on for the next six months, but after Terry's brother Marcus discovered their affair, he was forced to end their adulterous act, as he was livid to discovered what his brother and his best friend's wife were up to, and demanded that an end be put to their deception. Terry honoured his brother's request, as he knew that an exposure of their affair could generate an awful lot of hurt for more than just two people.

Chapter 3

When Terry walked into the restaurant, he could see Mr. and Mrs. Bradley and Cheryl sitting at a table that was situated at the back of the room. He thought Cheryl must have requested that particular table out of fear of reprisal from her dad, thinking they would be isolated from the rest of the diners. Terry felt a sudden urge to use the toilet. His stomach did a somersault, his mouth became dry from fear, and he could feel his knees shaking. He approached the table tentatively. Cheryl gave him a smile. Mr. Bradley didn't look up and did not acknowledge Terry's presence. This was the man who thought that he was good enough to marry his precious daughter, and he wasn't about to make life easy for him until he proved that he was good enough.

Mrs. Bradley stood up as he approached them. 'You must be Terry!' she said with delight. 'Nice meeting you!'

He felt uncomfortable, since Mr. Bradley still hadn't acknowledged him.

'Hi, Mr. Bradley,' said Terry. Mr. Bradley looked up at Terry without responding.

'Take a seat,' said Mrs. Bradley, trying to distract Terry from her husband's behaviour. 'Cheryl has told me all about you. I recognize you from church,' she added.

It was half an hour later before Mr. Bradley broke his silence. 'So what qualities do you possess that make you think you're good enough for my daughter?' he asked sternly.

Terry was taken aback; he had anticipated some difficult questions from the man, but he didn't expect the first to be so direct.

Four hours later, after they had finished their dessert, Mr. Bradley appeared more amenable. *Maybe he was just hungry, so he came across as being an angry old man,* Terry thought to himself. Or maybe the future plans that I just outlined for Cheryl and me were pleasing to Mr. Bradley, muttered Terry to himself.

Terry had crossed the first hurdle successfully, but he knew that he wasn't out of the woods—he would be the most-scrutinized man in the town of Leicester. About this, he was right. The Bradley's kept a close eye on the engaged couple for the next year, prior to their marriage.

Terry wasn't what you would call intellectually astute, but he was a very hard worker; he would spend long hours in the library, five days a week, studying and finishing his university assignments. He would meet up with Cheryl at the hospital library, since he didn't have access to her university library, nor did she have access to his. Soon they became study partners, and through this, they were able to openly spend more time together.

Cheryl finished university before Terry, since her program for becoming a pharmacist was shorter than Terry's medical studies. She got a job working in one of the NHS's pharmacies straight after finishing university. Her job entailed attending weekly ward rounds, where she would review medications that were prescribed for patients, and advise medical staff on the selection and effects of drugs. She also held a weekly educational session, during which she would educate patients about their treatments and the benefits and adverse effects of the medications they were on.

Terry and Cheryl were a very loving and committed couple, and they had passion enough for each other to cause a volcano to erupt. He had also become her best friend over the years, and they would spend hours talking about everything from politics to fashion, and of course, their plans for the future. She felt safe and self-assured whenever he was around her because he was extremely supportive of her. He helped her to believe in herself immensely, and would encourage her to take on challenges that she thought were above and beyond her abilities. It was Terry who encouraged her to apply for the pharmacy post at such a public corporation as the NHS; Cheryl had wanted to apply for a post at a little community pharmacy out of fear that the NHS pharmacy post would be too challenging for someone who had no experience. Terry was now a Specialist Registrar (SPR) and with Cheryl employed full-time, they decided to get married and take out a mortgage on a house.

One thing that Cheryl and Terry had in common was a love for a stylish and lavish lifestyle. Cheryl didn't have much money, since she had only just started to work, but Terry came from a long line of wealth. His grandparents were wealthy business owners who had left him and his brothers enough money in their trust funds to make them millionaires.

Whilst Cheryl helped with the financing of the wedding, it was agreed upon that he would be solely responsible for putting the deposit down on their house. The only conflict came when Cheryl decided that she wanted to remain in Leicester, so that she could remain close to her parents and sister. Cheryl had never lived away from home and found the prospect of moving out to start a home with Terry daunting. However, she felt that if she lived close by her family, this would provide her with the best of both worlds—she would be able to live with the man she loved and adored, but would still be able to see her mom, dad, and sister on a regular basis.

Cheryl was quite close to Trinny, since there was only a year apart in age. They grew up sharing everything from clothing to make-up tips. It was Cheryl who was there, in the labour room, with Trinny when her first baby, Hannah, was delivered. That was the most frightening experience that Cheryl had ever encountered, yet also the most exciting and joyful. Trinny had gone into labour two weeks earlier than expected.

Cheryl had stopped by Trinny's home for a visit, as she had done on several occasions. When she got there, she noticed that Trinny was looking a bit off-colour.

'You look pale,' she said when Trinny opened the door.

'I was doing some cleaning and think that I may have overdone it—I'm in pain,' she replied.

'Pain!' bellowed Cheryl. 'Are you sure you're not in labour?'

'I'm not due yet,' she replied.

Before Cheryl had a chance to reply, she followed Trinny's eyes and saw that she was standing in a puddle of brown fluid that had just run down her feet.

'I think my water …' she looked up at Cheryl and began to search her face for answers.

Cheryl stared back with a look of 'tell me it isn't so.'

'Donovan … Donovan! He's going to miss the birth of our firstborn,' screamed Trinny, making reference to her husband.

Donovan was a lorry driver, transporting goods to supermarkets around the country. He'd sometimes stop over in London when he had a busy schedule there, and this could sometimes last for an entire week before he'd return home. He had booked the next two weeks off from work in anticipation of the birth, and neither of them had imagined that the baby would arrive before Donavan's return home, as he had given himself enough time to prepare for the birth, or so he thought.

It was said that for first-time mothers, their babies were always late. This they believed to be true, since Trinny herself hadn't arrived on time and was late by eight days. Donavan was his parents' firstborn, and he, too, was late.

'Let's not forget to mention Aunt Doris, who was so late in delivering Sasha that she had to be induced,' emphasised Cheryl. 'I'll give Donovan a call. In the meantime, pack your bag whilst I ring the ward to inform them that you're coming.'

The contractions suddenly started coming at what seemed like the later stage of labour, rather than the first stage. This wasn't textbook labour, and everything that Trinny had read about and learnt from her midwife all seemed to be in vain now.

Cheryl managed to get Trinny to the hospital, where she became so frantic that when she got to the labouring ward, one nurse looked at her with a look of 'you should be on a psychiatric ward, not here.' It took another fourteen hours before little Hannah was born. Hannah was born at 6.15 hours and weighed a healthy eight pounds. She was the spitting image of her dad, Donovan: full lips, a pointy little nose, and little, screwed-up eyes. She was covered in various fluids that must have helped to protect her throughout the duration of her stay in her mother's womb, of which wasn't a beautiful sight. But beneath that gruesome layer, layed a gorgeous baby girl. She took Cheryl's breath away.

By this point, Cheryl was half-naked, since Trinny had pulled at her clothing every time she felt a contraction. Cheryl had never witnessed anyone in so much pain, and she promised herself that for her own labour, she would request horse tranquilisers.

Chapter 4

Terry wasn't happy about living locally, since the houses didn't quite meet his standards. He had his heart set on moving to Hertfordshire, where he believed the houses to be grander and the neighbourhoods more affluent. They had their first pre-marital row about this, the resolution being that Terry went along with Cheryl's wish.

Round one to the Bradleys! she thought.

They decided to look to buy a five-bedroom, detached in Stony Gate in Leicester. The drive through the neighbourhood was breathtaking. On each side of the road there were green trees, which seemed to ascend to the sky for at least two miles. There were a few oast houses, which gave the area the look and feel of the country. Whilst Terry was keen on modern buildings and newly built neighbourhoods, Cheryl had a love for the country life, since she had always associated the country life with an affluent way of living, something that had evaded her and her family whilst she was growing up.

On the right, just as they turned onto Street Boulevard Drive, where they were about to view what just might be their first home, the houses were exquisite. There, the elongated buildings and their décor had the appearance of mansions. Cheryl wished that the house that they were about to view would be as beautiful, but she knew that they wouldn't be able to afford anything as magnificent. She was a newly qualified pharmacist, and Terry was still a junior doctor, and the amount of savings they had could not allow them such a lifestyle. Well, that's what she thought.

Cheryl reacted with sheer excitement when she realized that one of her dreams was to become a reality. Terry was by far less excited, as he'd grown accustomed to this way of life, having grown up and lived in a similar neighbourhood. He saw living in Leicester as remaining in the same social circle—or even as taking a step backward in life. He had hoped to climb the social ladder and buy a property somewhere more affluent.

When Terry pulled up on the left, directly in front of a massive black and gold iron gate, which was the entry to a detached bungalow that looked like a cottage, Cheryl's heart sank.

'Here you are, Mrs. Odazic!' he said jeeringly to his wife-to-be.

'Is this it?' moaned Cheryl. She could hardly disguise her disappointment.

'It's the closest you'll ever get to the type of houses in Hertfordshire,' he said sarcastically.

Cheryl could detect a sense of a grudge in his voice, and she could feel the anger building up inside; it was like a tornado twirling around as it builds to gather enough strength and speed to destroy everything in its path. She opened her mouth to demolish the obstacle in her path, but suddenly, she stopped. She remembered that it was Terry who had the cash, and was it not for him, she wouldn't be able to achieve her dream. After all, she was from a working-class background and was lucky to have met a man like Terry, she told herself.

She gave him a forced smile, and as she turned in the direction of the house, he blurted out, 'Did you take me seriously?'

Cheryl turned around to see Terry laughing at her. 'Is this not the house?' she asked.

'I'll buy a bungalow when I'm old and grey!' he said mockingly.

Cheryl sighed a sigh of relief, and as they headed back to the car, she held Terry's hand. He returned the gesture by rubbing her hand between his. Four houses down the road, they could see a car marked 'Jackson Grundy,' and Cheryl knew that the house that they were about to view must be one of the last two on their right, since the car of the estate agent who they were about to meet was parked in between the two.

As they drew closer, she felt a a twinge of ambiguity, since the two houses where the estate agent's car was parked in front of, were as grand as the houses they had seen earlier, and liked, as they drove through the neighbourhood. She knew Terry had a bit of money to spare, but she didn't know exactly how much. He had just told her that his grandparents had left him some cash in a trust fund, but he hadn't disclosed how much.

When they pulled up behind the estate agent's car, Cheryl looked at the two houses, but dared herself not to dream or hope that one of the two of them could potentially become her new home.

'Hi. Mr. and Mrs. Odazic, is it?' queried this short, stocky man, dressed in a black suit and tie and an off-white shirt, in a local accent.

'You must be Henry!' replied Terry, as he stretched his arm out to greet the man. 'This is my other half,' said Terry, pointing to Cheryl.

Cheryl looked at both men with anticipation, eager to hear which of the houses they were about to view, if either.

'This is the house in question,' said Henry, pointing at the house to their right. Cheryl gasped and reached out for Terry's arm, having become faint from the anxiety that was building inside her, and the shock at discovering that such an opulent house was about to become hers.

Terry noticed her reaction and became concerned. He grabbed hold of her waist and pulled her to him so that his body was able to support hers. 'What's the matter?' he asked, concerningly.

'I feel a bit faint,' she replied. 'It must be all the stress and excitement of getting married and house-hunting,' she further replied. 'I feel okay now.'

Terry sat her in the car and carried out a quick examination of her. 'You look okay,' he said with a smile. 'But I think we should call off today's viewing; you're clearly tired.'

'No, no,' screamed Cheryl. 'Let's not jump ahead of ourselves. I'm fine, and we don't have plenty of time left, as the date of the wedding is fast approaching.'

They continued with the viewing, with Terry keeping a close eye on Cheryl. The house had a drive big enough to hold at least twelve cars. It was a detached, but not the kind of detached house that Cheryl was familiar with. It was a far cry from the red-brick, two-story houses that Cheryl knew.

Not only was this detached not red-brick, but it also had massive windows that mirrored those of Terry's family home, and the houses they had passed on their way in—only they were also much bigger and seemed more posh. *Maybe it's the style, the décor, or even the shape, but they are definitely more posh,* she thought to herself.

When they opened the front door, they were greeted with a patio the size of Cheryl's old room in her parents' home. Her mouth fell open, her eyes got wider, and she was speechless. The plushest houses she had ever seen so far were Terry's and that of a classmate of hers back when she was in university. Siara had invited a few of them from university to her house so that they could work on a group presentation due the following week. Cheryl and the others had all gasped when they walked in. They had never before entered a house of such magnitude or reeking of such wealth. Cheryl hadn't known what Siara's parents did for a living, but they were clearly not an ordinary or average family.

The door off the patio led them into a room that was big enough to accommodate their entire wedding-guest list. Situated at the right side of the room was a grand staircase with a spiral banister. As they made their way to the top floor, Cheryl uttered, 'This is breathtaking.'

Although Terry would have loved to have lived elsewhere, he was thrilled to see Cheryl's reaction to the house. He wanted to make her happy and give her anything that she wanted; by buying this home, he was taking the first step in achieving that. He had a proud expression on his face as they both took in the view.

'Are you impressed?' he asked Cheryl after they had viewed the upstairs and were on their way back downstairs.

'Can we afford this?' she whispered, not wanting to be embarrassed should the estate agent overhear their conversation.

'Do you like it?' asked Terry.

'Yes … but …'

'No buts,' Terry interrupted. 'Do you like it?' he asked forcefully.

'Yes.'

'Do you want it?'

Cheryl looked at him with a perplexed look. 'Surely we can't …'

Terry once again interrupted her sentence before she could finish. 'Cheryl, answer my question. Do you want this house?'

'Yes,' she said nervously.

'Consider it yours!'

They followed the estate agent back to his office, and the process of taking over ownership for this magnificent house began. As they walked out of the estate agent's office, Terry scooped Cheryl into his arms. 'I will do whatever it takes, Mrs. Odazic, to make you happy. Anything! You name it, and you've got it!'

Cheryl was lost for words; she couldn't express what she wanted to say to Terry, and tears trickled down her cheeks. She forced herself out of his hands to give him an embrace, but she landed awkwardly on one foot, and her shoe's high heel got stuck in a drain cover. Terry reached down to try and release her foot, but the shoe wouldn't release from the drain cover.

'Take your foot out of the shoe!' Terry demanded.

'But these are my most expensive shoes,' she bellowed.

'The shoe is stuck, Cheryl. You'll just have to take your foot out, expensive or not!' He tried to release her foot, but Cheryl pressed against his weight. 'Get your bloody foot out, Cheryl!'

He was spitting fire at this point, because he couldn't believe Cheryl was determined to lose her foot along with what she called her most expensive shoes, as she seemed determined not to release her foot from her shoes, and would rather have her foot stuck in the shoe, if she wasn't able to get her precious shoes unstuck. But Cheryl continued to resist—she had paid close to eighty pounds for her pair of shoes, and she wasn't ready to lose one to a drain cover without a fight.

Terry leapt from his stooping position and stood upright so his stare could meet hers. 'Cheryl, I just bought you a house for half a million pounds, so surely I can replace these cheap-looking shoes!'

'Eighty pounds, eighty pounds, eighty pounds!' she screamed. Terry took out his mobile phone and dialled 999.

'Hello, this is the emergency service. Which emergency service do you require?' a voice said on the other end of the line.

'The police, ambulance, fire … ! Whoever can get my wife's foot and shoes …'

Cheryl released her foot from her shoe upon hearing this.

'Sorry to bother you. It seems a passerby has helped.'

Cheryl was panting from the anxiety of losing her precious shoe, and Terry was panting from the exhaustion of trying to release her foot from it, combined with his anger.

'That's an eighty-pound pair!'

Terry reached into his pocket and pulled out his wallet, which was filled with clean, new notes. 'Here's two hundred pounds; go and buy yourself two more pairs of eighty-pound shoes!' he said quite angrily, as he pushed the money into Cheryl's hands.

He regretted uttering these words as soon as they came out. Cheryl pulled her hands back, and the notes fell to the ground. To her, this was an insult. Here was the rich boy, who'd just bought her a house that would have remained only in her dreams if he hadn't. *What was eighty pounds to him? Change for sweets*, she thought. She was hurt by his gesture and felt undermined by him.

Terry made his way back to the car, but Cheryl refused to follow. She turned in the direction of the bus stop. Terry saw her but decided to ignore her because he wasn't just angry; his ego was bruised as well. Here he was, about to marry her, and she was bothered about losing a pair of eighty-pound shoes when he could more than afford to replace them. *Does she not believe in me?* he wondered.

Cheryl was so embarrassed and angry that she forgot that she was wearing only one shoe. If it had not been for a group of school boys who stopped to stare at her as she went by on a single four-inch-heeled shoe, she wouldn't have realized that she was walking with a heavily lopsided gait that was attracting the attention of others.

She turned on her heel in an attempt to head back to their car, but Terry had sped off at high speed. She was distraught and, even more, embarrassed, and she scanned the shops around her in desperation to see if there was a shoe store, but there wasn't. So she took off the one shoe and headed, barefoot, for the bus stop, which was some half an hour away.

On her arrival home, her mother was astonished by her appearance: she was barefooted, and her face was stained with streaks of mascara from crying.

'What on earth happened to you?' she asked, thinking that Cheryl had been mugged. 'And where is Terry?' she asked in a high-pitched voice that emphasised her concern for her daughter.

Cheryl explained about her 'eighty-pound shoes.' Her mother was able to see the funny side, but Cheryl couldn't. She fumed about the manner in which Terry had thrown his money at her; she was angry that he had left her to make her way home on her own; she was mad at the unwanted attention she had received; but most of all, she was livid—*livid*—at how he had forced her to leave her shoes behind. To Cheryl, this was a lot of money, and whilst she considered herself fortunate to have more shoes than most people, this was one of the few pairs of expensive shoes that she owned.

Back home, Terry had calmed down and started to reflect on how cross he was with Cheryl. He felt guilty about the way he had thrown his money at her, and even more guilty at leaving her to find her way home with just one shoe.

The phone rang. 'Cheryl it's for you!' her mother hollered from the bottom of the stairs.

Cheryl picked the receiver up, hoping it was Terry. She wasn't disappointed. She felt that he had been dismissive of her feelings and somewhat condescending, but it was hard for her to stay angry at him. Behind his act of superiority, she felt loved, lots of love, and she knew that his actions weren't intended to hurt her.

'I'm sorry,' she said.

'No … no, I'm sorry,' Terry replied. 'I should have been more understanding.'

Chapter 5

The wedding was to be a very grand affair, with a guest list of well over three hundred people. Terry was from a very large family, and it would have been considered rude if he hadn't invited all of them. He had guests flying in from Syria and other parts of the world. Cheryl's family wasn't as large, but with her dad being the head of a church, it would have been viewed as snobbery, if they hadn't invited some of the members of the Church. She also had aunts, uncles, and cousins flying in from the Caribbean. No expense was spared since Terry was the last of his parents' three children, and they wanted to go all out for his wedding.

Even though Cheryl's parents weren't wealthy, they were able to help with some of the expenditures. Cheryl and Terry also participated in paying.

Attention was paid to every detail, with Cheryl scrutinizing and critiquing each aspect of her wedding day. She looked at the bridesmaids' outfits with a magnifying glass and must have asked for flower arrangements to be redone a hundred times. She had to be the coordinator, organizer, and planner.

'Can you rearrange the layout of the table?' she had ordered one of the wedding organizers. 'I'd rather the wine glasses be placed in the middle of the table, as opposed to where they are.'

The poor woman was left steaming, having spent the past day and a half trying to make the table arrangements impeccable, and now, here she was, ordered to rearrange more than three hundred glasses.

'Didn't know she could get to this stage in life,' expressed the woman, referring to Cheryl's poor background and her overnight move into a lifestyle of wealth, which she found unbelievable.

At the church, the cream and red flowers lined the entrance of the church and then continued down the aisle, along the pews, and across the rostrum of the church. The blessing was conducted at Cheryl's dad's church; however, he wasn't able to perform the ceremony because he played a key role in her wedding, giving her away. The blessing ceremony was attended by close friends and the families of the bride and groom; the invitation was extended to all the more than three hundred guests invited to the reception.

Cheryl was late arriving at the church, not because it was customary, but because she made such a fuss about everything, from her hair to her dress to her makeup. She complained that her hair was too wavy, and then it was too straight at the front. It seemed there was no pleasing her on the day. It took her sister's intervention to get her out of the house.

Back at the church, Terry had started to get anxious, because Cheryl was more than three hours late. *Is she having second thoughts?* he wondered. He was forced to remember the day her pricey shoe had gotten stuck in the cover of a drain and how cross he had gotten with her. *Could she have held a grudge against me for that?* he thought.

The sweat pouring down the side of his face was obvious enough for everyone to see. One woman joked that if he continued to sweat that profusely, they'd need lifeguards and a boat to get them out of the church.

The organ began to play, 'Here Comes the Bride.' Terry turned his head to see a beaming Cheryl being escorted down the aisle by her dad, who was dressed in a cream-colored, three-piece suit and matching shoes. He looked younger than his years, the tailored suit giving him a boyish look. This wasn't his usual attire, since he usually dressed more conservatively for his Sunday services. His jacket today was knee-length with an open back, as opposed to his typical, short-length jacket.

Cheryl looked immaculate. She was known to be a stunning woman, and today she looked lovelier than ever. As the crowd turned to look at Cheryl, their gasps could be heard travelling down the pew. She was simply breathtaking. She was dressed in an organza off-the shoulder gown, embellished with diamond studs. Her hair was pulled back in an elegant bun that emphasised her beautiful and strong features. She decided to break with tradition and did not wear a veil or tiara. She joked that she wanted to be able to see her husband clearly, without any obstruction. On her feet she wore a pair of Gucci shoes, a gift from her husband, which had a price tag of five thousand pounds.

Terry had asked Trinny to be his spy and inform him of the colour of Cheryl's dress so that he would be able to buy her a pair of matching shoes. He didn't want to run the risk of giving Cheryl the money to buy the shoes herself, because he thought that she wouldn't use all of the money for just a pair of shoes. He remembered too well the commotion she had made when her high heel had gotten stuck in the drain, and her apparent willingness to lose a foot along with the shoe.

Cheryl was amazed by the shoes that Terry had chosen for her. Although she didn't know how much they had cost him, she could tell by their style and quality that they were worth far more than the eighty-pound shoes she was accustomed to wearing. But as much as she loved the shoes, she wished that Terry had given her the money to purchase them herself, because with that sum of money, she would have been able to buy more than just one pair of shoes.

As she walked down the aisle on the arm of her father, Cheryl became overwhelmed, and her eyes filled with tears when her gaze met Terry's. She could see streaks of sweat running down the side of his face, which he wiped away with his handkerchief. She felt her heart do a somersault and her stomach tie up in knots. She turned to look at her dad to see his expression, and when she caught his eye, he gave a look that said it all—no words were needed.

Cheryl had seen this expression only a couple of times before. Once was when she had received her A-level report, earning two As and a B, and the other was at her graduation, when she was awarded a certificate for her pharmacy degree.

The walk down the aisle felt like the longest walk Cheryl had ever taken, since all eyes were focused on her. She walked tentatively, partly because she was nervous, and partly because she was about to embark on a journey that would see her living free from the guide of her parents for the first time. This she found exciting but daunting at the same time.

As they approached Terry, her dad released his arm from hers and tenderly transferred her hand into Terry's. This was a profound statement, as it proved that her dad had accepted her husband-to-be. It meant that her dad believed in his capabilities as a husband for her and, therefore, felt secure enough to entrust his precious daughter in his hands.

When the pastor took both their hands, he asked Terry to repeat after him the marriage vows to Cheryl.

'I, Terry, do take you, Cheryl, to be my …' His voice croaked, and he stopped to take a deep breath as he tried to fight back the tears.

Cheryl clasped his hand in both of hers, and began to rub it gently. He looked her in the eyes, nostrils flaring, lips quivering; he attempted to repeat his vows. ' … lawful wedded wife, to love and to cherish.' Still staring at her, he gasped for air. Tears had started to run down his face by now, and his nose had begun to produce snot. Cheryl tried to wipe away his tears, oblivious of her own, until she felt Terry wiping her cheek with his handkerchief.

'My makeup!' she whispered with a chuckle.

They stood there for minutes, just looking at each other and crying. When he resumed his vows, they noticed that there wasn't a dry eye left in the church. Everyone was touched by their love and happiness for each other and so, too, had begun to cry. Terry just managed to finish his speech through splutters of tears and snot.

Cheryl hadn't cried this much since she witnessed her sister giving birth to her firstborn. But this wedding day was the greatest day of her life by far. She was in a room with all the people whom she loved dearly: her mom, dad, sister, nieces and nephews, and the man whom she vowed to love 'until death do they part.'

They both looked a mess, Terry was covered in sweat, tears, and snot; Cheryl had her makeup smeared all over her face. Luckily, her sister was on hand to freshing her makeup before the photo shoot.

The photographer was a much sought-after after camera man; he was very gifted in his field and could make the most unattractive bride look stunning on her day. He had taken photos for several of Terry's family members during special occasions, and he was highly recommended to Terry. He came with a heavy price tag, but, according to those whom he had worked with, it was well worth it.

The photo shoot went on for what seemed like hours, because one of Terry's aunts hijacked the photo shoot. She wanted to be in most of the photos that were taken and seemed determined to take over the cameraman's role by instructing the guests how to pose. She started giving out instructions as to who should be snapped with whom, and at what angles they should stand. If she were left to her own devises, she would have had more photos taken of herself than of the bride.

Terry referred to her as Aunty Susie. Aunty Susie had the most beautiful hair that you could ever imagine—it was always immaculately styled and a strand was never out of place. But her hair was the only thing beautiful about her. She had a face that looked like a hyena's, and her neck was so short that her mouth appeared to be part of her chest. She was short and stocky, with a protruding stomach and an oversized waistline. She had a permanent frown that gave her an angry expression.

'On meeting her, I thought that she wasn't happy about our union, since she kept giving me this hostile look. This caused me to feel very uncomfortable in her presence, and I found her to be unwelcoming, but Terry put my mind at ease when he told me that this was Aunty Susie's natural expression,' Cheryl had told her sister. 'Her face is built at an angle; if she isn't smiling, then she just looks angry, he once told me. Terry said that his mother told him that their Grandpa and Grandma must have been having a fight when Aunty Susie was created.' The two women laughed.

Perhaps it was because of her physical appearance and the knowledge that the photographer had the ability to turn an ugly duckling into a swan, that made Aunty Susie so keen to have so many of her photos taken.

'Oh, can you not …'

Terry interrupted before Aunty Susie could finish her sentence. 'Aunty, leave the photographer to do his job; that's what he is being paid for. And if there's any problem, Cheryl or I will sort it out.'

Her angry expression had now become hostile, and she gave Terry a look that, if looks could kill, would have turned the wedding into a wake.

Cheryl was pleased that Terry had stepped in to defend their day, and was even more pleased that he had included her as one of the people who had the authority to call the shots. From then onward, the photo shoot was successful, since there were no more interruptions from Aunty Susie—or anyone else, for that matter. At the end of the photo shoot, Cheryl and Terry had two white doves released as a symbol of their love for each other.

The reception was held at Woburn Abbey, and the guests couldn't have made any more effort in their attire. They were so stylishly dressed that they gave the room the atmosphere of a fashion event. Cheryl had changed into a corset style lilac dress that hugged and accentuated every curve of her body. Terry sported black trousers, coupled with a lilac jacket and black shirt. Their outfits were coordinated as they strode past their smiling guests to take their seats at their designated table.

The menu items ranged from Afro-Caribbean to Asian dishes, which included Manish water, goat curry, salmon, rice and peas, somosas, biriani, and patties. Terry opted not to have any Syrian dishes, because he didn't find any of them particularly appetising. This had angered his mother because she felt that her son had snubbed her culture. 'You're a Syrian, and don't you ever forget that,' she scolded him.

Cheryl's dad was called upon to give a speech. It was evident that he not only approved of his new son-in-law, but that he also thought highly of him. He spoke of how he had always prayed for his daughters to be successful in everything that they did, and had always asked God to send them husbands from heaven. 'When my Trinny got married to Donnavan, I knew he was chosen by God, and today, I know that Terry has been sent from heaven above,' he declared.

Terry knew that Mr. Bradley was speaking from the heart, because this was the very man who had refused to even acknowledge him on the first day that they met. He could remember everything that he had said to him on that day, and if Cheryl wasn't special to him, he could have just ended the relationship there and then, because the man was so cold and rude toward him, that he had thought it would be impossible to have a successful relationship with his daughter. As he sat listening to his speech, Terry felt a feeling of accomplishment and happiness. He turned to look at Cheryl, who had streams of tears running down her face. Through her lifetime, she had loved only two men; Terry was one, and her dad, the other, and it meant so much to her, that each one had so much respect for the other.

Terry's brother Sullivan took centre stage to give his speech. He joked about how special Cheryl was to not only to Terry, but also to the entire Odazic family, especially since they thought that he would never get married because he was a playboy and lived a wild lifestyle, before he met Cheryl. 'Thank you for transforming his life. We can see how much he's changed since he's met you,' he further exclaimed.

Cheryl and Terry had the same response, each turning to look at the other. There was a twinkle in his eyes as he stared lovingly at her. He mouthed 'thank you' to her, and she responded with an 'I love you!' before reaching out to kiss him on the lips.

As their lips met, Terry's brother, Sullivan, shouted, 'Who said you could kiss the bride?'

The entire room, with roars of laughter, turned to look in their direction. Terry stood up and took Cheryl by the hand, pulling her to her feet. He pulled her to him so that her body was so close to his, that not even air could pass between them. He caressed her slender hips and stooped over to place his lips on hers. What ensued was a lingering kiss. The room broke out into further cheers, and everyone rose to their feet.

Terry looked up and scanned the room, and with a voice exuding pride, he announced. 'This is my wife, mine to love and to hold!' The room broke out in another wave of laughter, and some people began to shout, 'Hurray, hurray! Terry's got a wife!'

The guests and the bride and groom spent the night dancing to ballads and calypso music. Terry was a great lover of all types of music and could use his body to move to the beat of the music, to perfection. His dance movements were captivating; he became the centre of attention whenever he was on a dance floor, and tonight was no exception. He gyrated his hips to calypso music in a manner that made his hips appear as if they were mere springs. He spread his legs wide apart and bumped and grind all the way to the floor before coming back up again. His hips were moving as fast and as swift as a gig.

The DJ started to play 'Gimme Dollar,' which was a popular calypso song in the Caribbean back in the early nineties. 'Cent, five cent, ten cent dollar … gimme dollar …' When the song reached the chorus, 'gimme dollar,' Terry grabbed hold of Cheryl, forced her legs open with his, and started to move his hips back and forth in a sexual manner. He pulled her up onto his legs as he went down to the floor. She could feel him getting hard beneath her, and as he rubbed up and down against her clitoris, she could feel herself getting aroused. She wanted to tell him to stop because she feared that she wouldn't be able to control herself, but the music was so loud and the guests were so noisy that her efforts would have been in vain.

It had gone past midnight, and the reception was about to come to a close. The crowd was now thinning, and the guests were saying their good-byes. Some of them were packing goody bags of dinner leftovers. Others were climbing into their cars to make their way to their rooms in nearby hotels, whilst others had the long drive back to the different counties that they had come from. Some came from as far as Manchester; others, from Leeds. Cheryl was relieved now that all the years of keeping their relationship a secret from her parents, and most of those who knew them, had come to an end. They could now publicly declare their love for each other.

They had to make their way to Claridge's Hotel that night, since they had a plane to board from Heathrow Airport the following day. The drive would have taken them about an hour and a half from Woburn Abbey to the hotel during rush hour, but they anticipated it to be far shorter after the reception, since it had gone past midnight. They were both tired, and Cheryl's face looked drawn from the events, but nonetheless, they were both elated about the success of their wedding, and were looking forward to their life together.

As they clambered into the waiting limousine, Terry ordered the driver to take them to their destination. As she lay on the elongated seats of the limousine, with her feet resting in his lap, Cheryl joked about Aunt Susie and how she tried to hijack the photo session.

'Come along, Sullivan and Marcus, come and be photographed with Terry and your Aunt Susie,' Cheryl said in a high-pitched voice, trying to imitate the woman. She could now see the funny side of it, and laughed so much that she threw her legs in the air, hitting the ceiling of the limousine with her bare feet.

Chapter 6

Terry lifted her out of the limousine and carried her straight into their hotel suite. He tried to open their room door with Cheryl in his arms, but he stumbled as the door flew open. A loud thud could be heard as they fell to the ground.

'Sorry, Mrs. Odazic,' he said as he burst into fits of laughter. Their eyes met; she stared at him whilst breathing heavily. He kicked the door shut with his foot and started tearing at her clothes. She unbuckled his belt and pulled his trousers over his backside; he rolled from off her, with one hand caressing her firm backside, and the other guiding her on top of him. What Cheryl did next caused him to become paralysed with shock. In the three years that they had been dating, she had shown refutation about performing such an act. The first time Terry had used his tongue on her 'down below'; she had thought it was disgusting.

'Do people do that to each other?' she had asked, with a repulsed look on her face. And now, here she was, with him in her mouth. Her inexperience caused her to choke when she attempted to put the entire length of him in her mouth. It had gone only halfway when the tip of his penis clogged the back of her throat, almost cutting off her air supply.

Terry noticed what was happening but was unable to respond, since he was still frozen to the spot in disbelief. It was only when he felt her teeth digging into him, that he was able to move himself from his position.

'Ouch!' he screamed as he reached out to grab hold of her mouth. Cheryl pulled back in surprise, and he fell out of her mouth, floppy.

'Have you come already?'

'No, Cheryl, you almost castrated me!'

'I thought …'

He could see in her eyes her need to please him and suddenly remembered how innocent she was. He was her first love and her first sexual encounter; everything she knew about sex had come from him, and now she was ready to go a step further. It was up to him to teach her.

'No, darling,' he said as he stroked her cheek. 'Your teeth caught me,' he tried carefully to explain.

She became flushed with embarrassment and apologised profusely.

* * *

They boarded their flight to Jamaica to start their honeymoon the following morning. This was a gift from Cheryl's parents. It was a ten-hour flight, and they spent most of it sleeping, since they hadn't had time to rest before the wedding.

They arrived at Montego Bay Airport and were met by one of Cheryl's cousins, who had volunteered to escort them to their hotel. The sun was just rising; it was breathtaking. Plummeting out of the sky was a circle of bright orange and yellow luminous rays of light. It was difficult to look directly at the sun because it was so bright, that it was blinding.

Outside the airport terminal, the crowd of people and the noise that echoed from them gave the feel of being in a market. There were cars parked in an unorganised fashion, and men and women were leaning out of their car doors, shouting and beckoning to their loved ones. One woman jumped from her car, barefoot, and ran across the tarmac in an attempt to reach someone who had just landed with the newlyweds.

'Joane, se mi ya!' she shouted.

Terry looked puzzled and out of his comfort zone. He had travelled to many places, but he had never been to Jamaica, and whilst he was familiar with the dialect because he'd heard Cheryl's parents speak it occasionally, he'd never heard so much noise in a public place, not even in Leicester's market. There was music coming from every direction, from speakers as large as cars lining the streets. The only song that Terry could actually identify, was Bob Marley's 'No Woman No Cry.' The mixture of noises drowned out the actual words and tunes of the songs that were being played.

The temperature was soaring, and men walked around with no shirts, and some of the women were scantily dressed.

'What on earth is she wearing?' Terry questioned as a young girl went by them. She had on a midriff top that was so tight, it fitted her like a second skin; her shorts gave a new meaning to the word 'shorts,' and nothing was left to the imagination.

'That's called a batty rider!' giggled Cheryl.

'What does that mean?' quizzed Terry.

'See for yourself,' she said mockingly. The young woman turned around to see Terry staring at her.

'What yu looking at?' she asked with a frown.

Terry quickly manoeuvred his head to look in the opposite direction. He had gone bright red in the face and was now embarrassed. Cheryl had seen the funny side to it and was in stitches.

'You don't stare at Jamaicans without being challenged, darling, especially not in their own backyards,' she teased.

The drive from Negril to Ocho Rios was a long one, roughly eighty miles, and although they were tired, they relished every moment, since it gave them time to view and capture every aspect of the country's beauty. The scenery of the country was stunning; the natural resources of the country were well-preserved and attended to. It was easy to see why this part of the country was a favourite of tourists from across the globe. There were green hills that stretched for miles and miles on both sides of the road.

At the top of these hills were elongated palm trees that swayed in the wind, and the bright rays of sunlight and the sounds of the wildlife, gave the feeling of being in paradise.

The hotel was surrounded by a deep blue sea, which they could hear beating against the shores as the tide came in. The ocean varied in its mood—it was like it had bipolar disorder: the tide rose so high and powerful that it gave the feeling of a storm developing, and then it would become still and peaceful, yet enchanting.

It was a honeymoon filled with passion and lovemaking. This was the second time that Cheryl engaged in a sexual act with Terry without feeling that she was compromising herself and disregarding her morals. The first was back at the hotel in London where she almost casterate Terry. They could barely keep their hands off each other.

'You two must be newlyweds,' observed a man with a deep American accent.

'You remind me of my Brooke and me when we got married. It's been forty years to the day,' he expressed gleefully. 'That's impressive,' responded Terry. 'Three days as man and wife!' he further explained.

It was Cheryl and Terry's second morning in the breakfast lounge. And although they had ordered breakfast, they spent more time being attentive toward each other, than they did eating the food that was served to them.

The hotel's beautiful white sand and the blue sea helped to create a romantic atmosphere. One night, as Cheryl and Terry walked back from the bar to their hotel suite, they decided to sit on the beach and enjoy the beautiful weather. It had gone past 23.00 hours, and most of the hotel guests had retired to bed, with the exception of those who were out enjoying the nightlife. The temperature was soaring—it was 95 degrees—but resting on the beach, with its lovely palm trees swaying in the cool Jamaican breeze, was quite comfortable and relaxing.

As they lay watching the stars, Cheryl teasingly climbed on top of Terry's chest; she could feel his heart pounding under her slender body as he placed his hand in the small of her back. As she looked up to catch his stare, she knew that she had made the right choice in marrying him, and life with him would be rewarding.

'Have I ever told you how much I love you, Mr. Odazic? I'm about the luckiest girl alive! Thank you for loving me!'

He gazed into her big, dark brown eyes, and a chill swept his body. He was speechless and was unable to verbalise what he felt for her. He had been with many women, but none had captured his heart in the manner that Cheryl had. His body ached with passion; he could feel the adrenalin rushing through him, his heart pumping, and his thoughts were filled with words, but he was unable to express them. As Cheryl stared back at him, she could see him welling up. His face became bright red, and his eyes were filled with tears. For the next five minutes, they exchanged thoughts through non-verbal communication. Words weren't needed for any more expressions of love, since their eyes were able to pass on their emotions.

There were plenty activities and sight-seeing to do on the island. They took a tour of the White River, with its pristine, crystal-clear water. It was a three-mile journey that lasted for an hour and a half. The banks were lined with coconut plantations, bamboo groves, and exotic flowers. The tour went on to White River Valley Garden, which must have been the Garden of Eden in another lifetime. It was said to have over one hundred different species of flowers. It simply took their breaths away. Terry and Cheryl felt like Adam and Eve. The only drawback was that they weren't alone, since there were other guests and the tour guide with them, and they weren't allowed to parade around in the nude.

The couple feasted on Jerk Cuisine, a well known dish in Jamaica that is well sought after, especially in the tourist resort area of the country, and Terry loved it so much he asked one of the cooks for the recipe.

Chapter 7

Married life was fantastic. They both worked Monday through Friday, 9-5, so they both had the weekends to themselves and could plan their weekend breaks.

Terry loved to travel. Before he had commenced medical school, he used to spend most of his weekends catching the ferry and the Euro star in and around Europe. So after they were married, Terry and Cheryl travelled to Europe for romantic breaks quite frequently. She particularly liked Belgium because of its quality chocolates, since she was a chocolate lover and would eat at least three bars a day.

Her sister often teased her about the amount of chocolate she ate, and how she'd managed to keep a slender figure. 'Without the consummation of chocolate, you'd disappear!' she'd often joke.

Terry preferred France because of its delicious wines. Terry loved his drink. Before he married Cheryl, he'd spend his weekends travelling and roaming from one nightclub to the next. He would return home or to his hotel suite intoxicated in the early hours of the mornings. Because of this, his mother hated the weekends and wished they didn't exist. During the week, her son was a responsible, respectable professional, but on the weekends, he became a drunken rogue. He would justify his behaviour by telling her that his job was a stressful one, coming across so many very sickly patients, some of whom, who never lived to see the next day. So on weekends, he just wanted to forget about what his eyes had forced him to be a witness to.

Terry learned to become domesticated during his marriage and would help around the house. This was expected of him, since Cheryl had seen her own mother become a slave to her father, washing, cleaning, and always making sure that there was food on the table when he returned home from work or study, always ensuring that his shirts were neatly pressed. The collars of his shirts had to have a fold in the middle. The seam in his trousers had to be the same length and be in a straight line. And although her mom seemed happy in her marriage, Cheryl had resented this. She never understood why an intelligent woman, would give up her own career to further that of her husband. She saw her mom as not having an identity other than being Mrs. Bradley, and she'd promised herself as a little girl, that she would not be subjected to the same fate.

Cheryl had a particular memory that was poignant to this day. She could remember her mother with four different pots cooking on the cooker and a pile of clothes to be ironed; she was running back and forth, between rooms, in an attempt to carry out her duties. It was a hot summer day, one of the hottest Britain had ever encountered, as the country was experiencing a heat wave. Mom was sweating profusely as she checked on her pots, one after the other, pouring a bit of water into the rice pot that had gone dry, spraying some olive oil on her braising steak, checking that her vegetables weren't too soggy, and making sure her cobage fish was just the way Dad liked it. She had become red in the face and was panting and was clearly tired. All the while, Dad had sat in the living room, reading his Bible.

There must be a scripture in the Bible that says thou should treat thy wife like a slave, thought Cheryl, who was playing hide-and-seek with her sister, Trinny, in the dining area when they heard a thud.

'Mom!' screamed Trinny as they stood over her motionless body. Cheryl threw herself on her mother, who was on the floor.

'Call the ambulance,' their dad had demanded.

It turned out that Mom had collapsed from sheer exhaustion, having two young children to care for, a house to look after, and a husband who was too caught up in his own world to give her any support. Mom spent the next twenty-five years playing the dutiful wife and perhaps collapsed from exhaustion on other occasions, but she never mentioned it. That incident didn't change Dad much—he continued to do very little to help Mom around the house—but it had changed Cheryl's perception about what should constitute a marriage.

Chapter 8

Cheryl's friends were in awe of Terry, and he seemed to them to be the ideal husband. He was a gorgeous man with an athletic physique, he was clever enough to be a doctor, and he was from good stock. He was from a family that had money, some of which he had inherited. He had no reservations when it came to spending it on Cheryl, and would do anything to make her happy. Her friends cooed over his attentive and caring nature. He always offered to make her a drink or to prepare her meals; he encouraged her to put her feet up whenever she appeared to be tired. He was always buying her little gifts on his return from work or during their weekend breaks. He took the time to find out about her day after they'd been apart. He was sensual and passionate during lovemaking; he met her demands, gave into her wants, and granted her desires. The hairs on the back of her neck would stand up during lovemaking, since he took the time to ensure that she was having as much pleasure as he was; it was never about just him.

Terry was progressing with his studies and was one exam away from becoming a consultant. Cheryl felt so proud of him. He became the topic of her conversation with her friends. She never referred to him as Terry, but as 'my husband.'

'You can tell you're a newlywed,' her friend Simone once said to her.

Cheryl and Simone had been friends since high school, but whilst Cheryl was ambitious and career-minded, Simone felt that her place in society was to marry an affluent man and become a housewife and a mother. She couldn't understand why any woman would want to go out to work, when she could stay at home and have her man make provisions for her. She was the same age as Cheryl, early twenties, and was in her third pregnancy. Her husband ran a textile company and was wealthy enough to allow her to stay at home. She lived in a seven-bedroom detached and had a helper who did the laundry and the cleaning. In the early days of her marriage, she always spoke of her husband in high spirits. Cheryl would get irritated with her, as they would rarely talk about anything else. She'd once asked Simone what would become of her if her husband ran off with another woman, since she had seemed to make him her world and had nothing else to fall back on.

Simone's response had been astounding, 'End my life.'

Cheryl had made this comment with the hope of getting Simone to have a dream, beyond her husband, and was shocked at her lack of aspiration and ambition. But now, after six years of marriage, Simone hardly ever spoke about her 'husband' and would flinch when the topic was brought up.

Cheryl sensed that all was not well in the Simpson's household. It turned out that Simone's husband rarely came home, and when he did, he was irritable and hostile to her, and spent little time with the kids.

'He's been having an affair with one of his employees,' said Simone.

'Are you sure about this?' questioned Cheryl.

'I followed him one night, after his many excuses for not coming home, and there they were …' She paused in reflection, her eyes welling up, her lips quivering; she was flushed in the face.

Cheryl reached out and grabbed hold of her, and for a moment, they just held each other and cried.

'How and why did you get pregnant again?' Cheryl asked in amazement.

'Well … he'll never say no to a romp between the sheets, and I am just trying to save what's left of my marriage. After all, he's a good dad.'

'A good dad who spends little time with his kids, why do you stay?' Cheryl asked.

'Where would we go? I have little education, and I've never worked. He's our source of income.'

'You can start somewhere!' emphasized Cheryl.

'Like on a council estate!' fired back Simone with a tone of irritation to her voice. 'I can never provide for my kids the way he can. Look at our home. Look at the lifestyle we have been living. Let's be realistic, Cheryl. Would you give all this up because your husband was seeing another woman? If he dies tomorrow, I get it all! I'm his wife, remember.'

Cheryl was lost for words because she knew that Simone lacked ambition, but she came to discover that she also lacked dignity and self-respect. Or maybe she'd had it taken away from her, it was hard to tell. She couldn't contain herself, and by now was bursting with rage. 'I'm ashamed to be called your friend!' screamed Cheryl.

'Don't start preaching to me, pastor's daughter!' bellowed Simone. 'Take your gospel and head for the front door. It's been a long time since I haven't been to church!'

Cheryl was too angry to say another word. She grabbed her bag and car keys and left, slamming the door behind her. She cried all the way home. To witness how dependency had stolen her friend, was heart-wrenching. She couldn't help thinking that if her friend was able to make provisions for her children on her own, how different it would be for her. She reflected on her own life and thought how blessed she was. *A good enough salary, a high-flying husband who loves me. But if he chooses to go … then …* She stopped; she couldn't bear the thought of losing Terry.

Chapter 9

Cheryl noticed that her social circle started to become smaller now that Terry and she spent most of their time together. She'd go shopping, and he would tow along. Every outfit that Cheryl chose had to have Terry's approval. She didn't mind this, since she loved him and so wanted to please him. She thought that it was fantastic that Terry wanted to spend all his spare time with her.

Cheryl continued her regular shopping trips to Birmingham Shopping Centre, but instead of shopping with Angel, as she once did, she was now doing it with Terry. Birmingham was one of Cheryl's favourite shopping venues, because there were so many high street shops within and around it, and there was a variety of stylish clothes to choose from. She and Angel used to spend the day going from one shop to the other, then taking a trip to the library, and they would always visit Wood Bridge Road, which was known for its Asian meals. Cheryl use to love the girly shopping trips, and she particularly looked forward to those weekends because she enjoyed Angel's company so much. But since her marriage to Terry, she saw very little of Angel, partly because they travelled so much abroad, and partly because Terry didn't particularly like Angel. He thought she was a bad influence on Cheryl because of her dress-sense and her free spirit. Angel was unmarried and didn't really have a steady boyfriend; she dated several men, although not at the same time. Terry saw her as being loose.

Gradually, Cheryl began to lose her friends, since Terry didn't seem to like any of them and would make derogatory statements about each and every one of them. This would lead to arguments, because Cheryl would jump to her friends' defence. After all, she had known most of them since childhood, so she knew them well. Of course, it was upsetting to suddenly have the man that she loved speak harshly about them.

Cheryl's friends started to complain about Terry and would make comments such as 'he's controlling you.' This angered her, since she saw herself as a strong-willed woman who would never tolerate any form of abuse from her man. For them to make this suggestion, was accusing Cheryl of being weak, which she didn't think she was. She thought that they were jealous of her and started seeing her friends through Terry's eyes.

She tried to convince herself that she was better off not having Angel as a friend, now that she was a respectable, married woman, and a married woman had no business befriending a woman who didn't honour the sanctity of marriage. She also distanced herself from Simone, because Terry said that she had a negative view about men and it wouldn't do Cheryl any good to keep in touch with her. He thought she'd eventually view men in the same manner that Simone did, which could slowly destroy her own marriage. And quite readily, Cheryl agreed. And there was Macy, who was a successful married woman, but Terry thought she was too much older than Cheryl, and had a life long experience that would corrupt Cheryl.

Terry started encouraging her to form friendships with his friends and made every effort to make this possible. Initially, Cheryl welcomed the idea, thinking that he just wanted her to be happy, and had her best interest at heart.

However, the two people whom she decided that she was never going to lose contact with were her mother, Lyn, and her sister, Trinny. Her mother had been her rock from her childhood; she would deprive herself of an item just so that Cheryl and her sister could have their dreams come true. Cheryl trusted her implicitly; she was the steel that held them together as a family. Trinny was her confidante, a shoulder she could always cry on, someone who'd cry with her and for her. Cheryl was never particularly close to her dad, because she resented him for many things, but she loved him and knew that, in his own way, he loved her.

Initially, Terry didn't seem to mind the close relationship that Cheryl had with her mom and Trinny. They'd visit her mom on Sundays for their tea, and on other occasions, they'd invite her mom, dad, and Trinny for lunch. They got on well as a family; Terry always made that extra effort to make his in-laws feel welcome.

He and Trinny had grown close to each other and would banter with each other. They both shared a dry sense of humour and understood each other very well. He often joked that she was adopted, because she didn't look like her mom and dad, or Cheryl, for that matter. 'They must have gotten you from one of the missionaries, who often visited your dad's church,' he joked.

'Recessive genes, it's called, Terry. And you call yourself a doctor. Frightening!' she teased.

Cheryl did miss not having her girlfriends around, since she didn't have any thing in common with Terry's friends. They were all housewives and didn't really venture outside of their homes without their husbands, not even for shopping. Their conversations focused on their husbands and their household chores, and having numerous kids. On one visit to Terry's best friend, Naz, Cheryl was aghast at how primitive his viewpoints were for such an educated man.

Naz was a surgeon before becoming a successful businessman. He had a chain of restaurants in and around Europe. He was on his second marriage, his first wife having died from a brain haemorrhage. Rumours had it that she died from being hit in the head by Naz, who used her as a punching bag, because she was a self-made millionaire who wouldn't give up work to stay at home and cater to his needs. Meena, his second wife, used to be their hired help, and Naz married her eighteen months after the death of his first wife.

This is a place where only the affluent can live, thought Cheryl as they drove through the neighbourhood on the way to their first visit to Naz's. The houses were mansions and were opulent enough to house royalty. When they got to a high iron gate, Terry got out of his car to press the button, and the gate opened slowly. At the house, they were met at the door by a young, attractive woman who had a little girl, with tightly curled black hair, holding onto her skirt. A baby was cradled in her arms, lying across her chest with his little chubby hand pulling at her blouse, as if to say 'Mummy, give me milk.' The woman was pleasant and welcoming and directed them to the front room.

The house had a regal feel to it. Not only was it unbelievably clean and tidy, but also the immaculate designs of the furniture and decor, must have been created with royalty in mind. It was grand, to say the least. Cheryl wondered how a household with two babies could be this clean and organised. The cushions were fluffed, and not one of them was out of place; they were neatly lined up in a row. The rugs were spotless, and even the ornaments that were in reach of the kids, were neatly in their places. There were no toys to be seen.

'How do you manage to keep such a spotless house, with two babies?' quizzed Cheryl.

Naz immediately emphasized that it was his wife's doing, as if to abolish any thought that he could ever be that domesticated.

They could smell a mixture of scented herbs coming from the kitchen,

'Something smells nice, Meena!' said Terry, licking his lips with his tongue.

'I'm cooking your favourite dish,' said Meena gleefully.

'Yum, yum!' responded Terry.

'What's that then?' asked a displeased-looking Cheryl.

'Byriani.'

'Oh? It's not roast beef!' squealed Cheryl reproachfully.

Terry didn't wish to hurt either woman. He could see that Cheryl had become riled, because he had always told her how much he loved her cooking, and that her roast beef was his favourite dish. And now she'd learnt that another woman prepared his favourite meal. He didn't want to disappoint Meena, since she was a friend, and had cooked for him on numerous occasions when he had visited Naz. He was stuck between a rock and a hard place.

Naz could see the anxiety in his friend's eyes and interrupted. 'So, Cheryl, what do you think of Hampshire?'

Meena rushed off to the kitchen with her baby in her arms when a whiff of burnt meat came through to the front room. Shaz, the older child, stayed to play with Cheryl's handbag, having developed a fascination with it, not putting it down since their arrival.

The smell of soiled diapers swept through the room. Cheryl was astounded at what occurred next.

'Meena, Shaz needs attending to!' shouted Naz. 'And could you make us all a drink? Orange juice for Cheryl, and something stronger for me and Terry!'

It was clear to see that this woman was struggling, and the man that helped to create these children, refused to give a hand in keeping them clean and fed. Meena rushed from the kitchen, where she was trying to cook a meal, to the bedroom in an attempt to change her toddler's nappy, and then she scurried back to the sitting room, where they had congregated. She was also trying to feed her baby, who was screaming his lungs out. He was clearly hungry, but maybe he was also feeling too hot from being in the kitchen with his mother. It was like a furnace in that kitchen, with the heat that was being produced by the cooker, and the spices were so hot, they sent Cheryl into a coughing fit, as it was a mixture of chilli powder and hot Jamaican pepper, a combination of which had always affected Cheryl when used at her mother's house.

What about that poor child? thought Cheryl to herself.

Meena had kept the baby with her since it was obvious that he wouldn't have had much, if any, attachment to his dad. *He's not a hands-on dad,* Cheryl thought.

This scene reminded her of her mother on the day that she collapsed from sheer exhaustion. Cheryl could feel herself getting angry, and just couldn't stand by and watch the manner in which Meena was being treated any longer, and offered to give Meena a helping hand. *But that is probably expected of me,* she thought.

She had wondered why such a successful man married a woman who was considered to be out of his caste, but now she could see the reason behind their union. After all, Naz wasn't looking for a wife to be his equal; he wanted a woman to bear him kids and do as she was told. She felt contempt for this man whom she barely knew, and felt that he should never have had the privilege of having a wife and family. In Cheryl's eyes, Naz was nothing but an abuser. He may have been the breadwinner for his family, but he was a mere pimp, and Meena would probably have been better off on the streets. *There she would have at least had a break when her clients went home to their wives,* she thought.

She challenged Terry about Naz's behaviour on the way home. She had been disappointed that Terry hadn't discouraged his friend's behaviour and encouraged him to be more of a help to Meena.

'It's not your place to interfere in other people's private affairs, Cheryl. You're there as a guest, not as a bloody social worker,' said Terry in a raised voice.

Chapter 10

Terry and Cheryl began thinking about starting a family. She preferred to wait another year, because there was a supervisory position at work that was promised to her, and becoming pregnant would have jeopardised this. She expressed her concerns to Terry. He didn't support her idea and thought that it was selfish to put aside starting a family because of her career. She decided to pass on the promotion that was promised to her, because she really wanted to become a mother, but, more importantly, she didn't want to go against Terry's wish.

What difference will a year make? I can get a promotion after I have my baby, she told herself.

So Terry and Cheryl decided to start trying for a baby. They spent the next two months putting measures in place to make this happen. Cheryl would wait to see if her cycle would come, and when it did, she was bitterly disappointed. She had bought an assortment of pregnancy test kits, and would test her urine at least three times a day out of desperation and excitement.

One day, just as Terry had pulled out of her, Cheryl rushed to her dressing table and pulled out a drawer. She reached for her clear blue kit, rushed to the toilet, and held it between her legs so the entrance to her vaginal canal, was sitting immediately above the kit. Before she could pass urine, she could feel his bodily fluid and hers dripping onto the kit. 'Oh hell,' she muttered, rushing off to replace the kit with a fresh one, because she believed that the kit with their bodily fluids was contaminated and, therefore, wouldn't give an accurate reading. As she waited in anticipation of seeing two pink lines appear, her heart began to race. She couldn't bear to look, so she called Terry to be the reader.

He was baffled. 'Are you expecting that the sex we just had … ?'

'Give me the kit,' interrupted Cheryl as she snatched it from his hand. 'I'm doing this for us!'

The following month, Cheryl was late seeing her cycle, her stomach had become distended, and she was convinced that she was pregnant. Her stomach visibly bulged more than usual.

'I don't understand. Why would I be showing already?' she asked, perplexed, whilst unwrapping another pregnancy kit. To her dismay, it showed only one pink line. She unwrapped another, and then another, both of which came back negative. Terry tried explaining to her the possible causes, but she refused to accept his explanation and made an appointment to see her doctor.

'I'm afraid, Mrs. Odazic, that the body does this. You see, when you've been on the pill for a while and then stop, the body does goes through changes as it adjusts to life without the pill.'

'You didn't need to see a doctor—that's what I had explained to you,' said Terry in a riled voice.

* * *

'Can I speak to Dr. Odazic please?'

'Whose calling?' questioned the voice on the other side of the phone?

'It's his wife.'

'Hi darling!' she greeted Terry as he took the receiver.

'What have I done to deserve this honour?' he said teasingly.

'I have the best news ever!' she exclaimed.

There was silence after Cheryl had made this statement; they could both be heard breathing.

'Are you …'

'I've got two pink lines. We're having a baby, darling!' she screamed.

Cheryl could hear him crying over the phone as he muttered 'I love you' to her.

It was a bittersweet moment for Cheryl. She was ecstatic that she was about to become a mother, but she was also sad, because she had only a few people to share her joy with, having lost all her friends. Terry must have made hundreds of phone calls to his nearest and dearest. For the first time in her marriage, Cheryl realised how alone she was. She started to reflect on how isolated her child would be from her family, and how he or she wouldn't know any of her friends, if she continued on the same path her marriage was taking her, as she had become isolated from her friends and family as her marriage to Terry progressed, even though most of them were living in the same county.

Terry was fantastic throughout her pregnancy. He would take time off from work to ensure that he was with her for all her antenatal appointments. He made sure that she was getting enough rest by trying to do most of the house chores himself. And he'd even take time off work to be by her side if she looked off-colour or got ill.

Her pregnancy wasn't a difficult one because she maintained good health throughout most of it. However, she did encounter little mishaps here and there. She woke up one morning to find that she was passing blood when using the toilet. She panicked, as she knew the possible implication of this. She screamed for Terry, who was frightened by the terror in her voice. As he approached her, he could smell her fear. He rushed her to the hospital, where she spent the night under close observation. The doctors had informed them that spotting during pregnancy was quite common, and occurred when there was a rupture of the umbilical cord. However, they wanted to rule out any other causes, so they thought it was best if she spent the next twenty-four hours under their care. That night, Terry didn't sleep; he sat next to her, observing her baseline. The nurses had become fed up with him by the morning, feeling that his interference was undermining their skills as practitioners.

Cheryl was fast approaching her due date, as she was now seven and a half months into her pregnancy, and had to take her maternity leave two weeks earlier than planned, since she was struggling with her back. Six weeks later, Cheryl had passed her due date by six days. She made an appointment to see her midwife and was told that the baby's head still hadn't moved into the labouring position.

'However, not to worry, not all babies are born with their heads descending first.'

Cheryl remembered the nurse at the antenatal clinic saying that babies who were born with their heads out first, made far quicker and easier deliveries, because there were fewer complications. She began to panic, her heart started racing. The thought of having her baby being dragged out from inside her with the aid of forceps was a frightening one, and it was something she hoped she wouldn't have to experience.

'So what's next?' she asked the midwife worriedly.

'I'll give you a few more days, and if you still haven't gone into labour, then we'll have to book you in a hospital to be induced.'

'Induced!' Cheryl bellowed. Her memory raced back to her antenatal sessions, and she again remembered the nurse explaining how painful it was to be induced. 'It's not a gradual process, like that of natural labour—the baby comes out with such force that it quadruples the level of pain.'

The midwife told Cheryl that she could encourage the birth of the baby by walking. It felt uncomfortable to do so, since the weight of the baby was now crushing her pelvic bone and aggravating her back pain. She became frustrated because she was in so much pain, and felt like she was losing control of how she'd planned her pregnancy and delivery to be.

Cheryl was a very organised woman, and would plan out every aspect of her life, such that, certain things had to be done on a specific day of the week, and had to be done a particular way. Her diary and her calendars were all filled in with red, green, and blue markers, where she would make little notes to remind herself of what was to be done and by when and how. Things rarely went wrong for Cheryl, as she would always have an alternative measure drawn up, just in case. However, on the few occasions when her plans hadn't materialised, she turned like an iguana, standing still whilst giving everyone around her an intimidating look, causing fear in some people and anger and irritation in others.

* * *

Trish was a committed and very focused staff member who was employed to work as an auxiliary on the ward that Cheryl was linked to as a pharmacist. She was responsible for setting up the laptop with the subject that would be discussed for the day, as well as being in charge of informing the patients about the topic that would be discussed during the session and making arrangements for them to attend. She had always succeeded in carrying out what was required of her, until one unfortunate day. The laptop malfunctioned; it wouldn't display the subject matter that was to be used as the topic for the day. Trish had spent so much time rushing around, trying to get help to rectify this problem, that she had forgotten to inform the patients whom she had booked in, that they would be running behind schedule. She made several attempts to inform Cheryl of the problems she was encountering. But every phone call that she had made to Cheryl's base on that day, had been in vain.

'I'm afraid Cheryl is not at the base at the moment. We're expecting her in the next ten minutes.' 'Oh, she's rather busy at the moment. Can I take a message?' These were a couple of the messages that were relayed to Trish.

Eventually, Cheryl arrived on the ward. She tried to enter the room, just like she had always done on her previous teaching sessions, but instead of walking into a room filled with eagerly waiting patients, and a laptop displaying the topic for the day, to her dismay, the room door was locked. She attempted to open the door again, bemused, but was again denied entry. The door had a little window at the top that was wide enough to be able to see anyone who was seated directly in front of it. When she peered through it, although a chair was visible, it was just an empty chair. She headed toward the office with a perplexed look and a defiant step in her stride.

'Oh Cheryl,' said Trish apologetically. 'I've been trying to get a hold of you, but to no avail.'

'Why is the room locked? And what are you doing standing here, when you should have been engaging the patients until ...'

Trish interrupted. 'The computer isn't working.'

'It was last week,' Cheryl said indignantly. 'Anyway, that's not an excuse. If it's not working, you get another one,' she screamed.

The office was filled with nurses and doctors, and they all turned in disbelief to look at Cheryl. It was unprofessional of her to rebuke her colleague in such a public manner, but this didn't stop her.

'No wonder you're just an auxiliary, and you can't even do that properly!'

Trish was fuming with anger, and so was her manager. She might be only an auxiliary on the ward, but she was one of the best workers she'd ever employed and was quite capable of carrying out her duties. The patients liked her, and her colleagues respected her as a person and a professional.

'Can I have a word with you, Cheryl?' the manager said with vigour.

'That can wait,' screamed Cheryl.

'Can I have a word with you, Cheryl? Now!' the manager demanded.

* * *

Cheryl had attended antenatal lessons and had followed the midwife's instructions as if she were following a recipe manual. She had endlessly researched the internet for guides to a swift delivery. And she was convinced that it would all go according to plan. Now, though, here she was, about to make the most important journey of her life, and she had little control, if any, of the outcome.

'Let's try and at least walk around the block,' Terry said cautiously to his wife.

It pained her to accept that he was right. Terry had always instructed his wife to do more activities during the later stage of her pregnancy, in an attempt to make her delivery a speedier one. The only time Cheryl ever walked during her pregnancy after her second trimester, was when she was at work.

'Lazy moms-to-be produce lazy babies,' he often teased her.

Cheryl put on her jogging outfit and her trainers and off she went with Terry. They made their way through their housing estate, taking the long way around. Cheryl was waddling, like she had been doing since she reached the seventh month in her pregnancy. She was slow on her feet because the weight of her stomach reduced her movements. She held Terry's hand as they strolled through the neighbourhood, taking in the views of the neatly kept gardens. She and Terry were a tactile couple and were often seen out together holding hands, but on this occasion, this wasn't a romantic gesture but a means of support.

'Wow! This neighbourhood is beautiful,' she exclaimed as they turned on Toronto Street. 'What area is this?' she asked Terry inquisitively.

'This is our neighbourhood,' retorted Terry.

'This bit here is a part of our neighbourhood?' she questioned, pointing to the row of houses they were approaching.

'Yes,' said Terry. 'And how long have you lived here?' he said teasingly. 'It just goes to show how lazy you are—drive to work and then home. You'd even drive to the kitchen and toilet at home, if you could.'

She chuckled. 'Am I really that bad?'

Upon their return home, Cheryl was in agonising pain. Her feet were blistered from the heat from her trainers; her thighs had rubbed against each other due to the amount of weight she had gained and were so sore that she felt like the top layer of her skin had come off; her pelvic area ached far more than it had ever done; and her back was so painful that she felt as if she'd been hit by a baseball bat. She could hardly lift her feet to enter through the patio door and had to be aided by Terry.

'I'm in agony,' she exclaimed.

'This is mild compared to labour, dear,' replied Terry in a teasing manner.

'Don't you patronise me, you insensitive …!' She stopped midway in her sentence, when she felt a pain shoot through her pelvic area. Terry looked concerned when he saw the grimace on her face.

'Are you all right?' he asked.

'Course I'm not, that's a darn stupid question!' She could feel herself getting angry, especially at Terry. She didn't want to be angry at him and couldn't understand why she felt so much anger toward him. *He's been very supportive; after all, he's just taken me for a walk*, she thought. Then it registered: As fantastic as he had been, he didn't know what it was like to be with child, and that was an experience that he would never know. He couldn't sit with her and say, 'Oh, that's how I felt when I was pregnant,' or 'Try doing this instead of that.' This was something she could discuss only with a woman; she needed a woman's empathy. She wanted her female friends— they'd all gone through it before her, some of them once, some twice, and some even three or four times. But she had none; she had disposed of them, at her husband's request. However much he tried to understand, it would never be the same. He tried giving her his advice, but it was all advice taken from a medical manual. Sometime she felt like she was his patient. *It really takes someone who has gone through an increase in dress size;*

whose breast size quadruped from a D-cup to a H-cup; whose hair fell out in chunks; whose pelvic bone was pushed so wide apart it prevented her from walking with that graceful stride she once had to be able to understand, she thought. A strong feeling of resentment rushed through her.

'It was a joint decision for me to get pregnant. However, we aren't jointly feeling the discomfort and the pain,' she retorted. 'And not to mention this weight that I'm carrying around, how unfair,' she spluttered. Terry didn't respond—he dared not, seeing how much pain she was in.

'I'm going to have a bath to see if it helps.'

'Would you like me to run the bath for you, darling'?

'Don't feel put out on my account,' she responded.

Terry once again didn't respond, realising that Cheryl was now looking for a fight, and fighting with a pregnant woman was the last thing he wanted.

That night, Cheryl was awoken by a sharp pain. She wasn't sure what to make of it, since she thought it could be from the walk. It lasted for a few seconds before fading away. A few minutes later, it was back, and then it faded and came back again. She prodded Terry, who was sleeping next to her, in his side. 'Terry, I think I might be in labour.'

Terry jumped up from his sleep.

'In fact, I'm quite sure I'm in labour.'

'How can you be so sure?' Terry asked.

Cheryl explained to him what she had felt. 'The walk must have encouraged it, just as the midwife had said. Shall we call the hospital to inform them that we're coming?'

By now, Terry was as white as the clouds. His eyes were bulging out of his head, and he looked like a man having withdrawal symptoms from a crack addiction, the sweat starting to drip off his face. He had seen many women in labour; he had even helped to deliver babies quite confidently, but it was quite different when the baby that was about to be born was his own. He needed more than confidence to get him through this. He feared being on his own with her and preferred the company of nurses and other doctors.

I'm training to be a bloody surgeon, not a paediatrician, he thought.

Cheryl tried to jog her memory about what she had learnt in her antenatal lessons. *It's too soon; they'll only end up sending me back home. My contractions are too far apart.*

Sixteen hours later, Cheryl had given birth to a bouncing baby girl by emergency Caesarean, having developed complications during labour. The baby was gorgeous and was the spitting image of Cheryl. Terry, her mom, and Trinny were all at the hospital, but only Terry was allowed in with her in the theatre room. He looked as though he had just done ten rounds in a boxing ring with Mike Tyson. He had scratches and bruises all over him, not to mention the ripped shirt he was wearing.

'What on earth happened?' Cheryl asked in astonishment at the sight of her husband, who was always immaculately groomed.

'Can't you remember any of it?'

Cheryl was now baffled.

'You did this during labour, just before they decided to give a Caesarean.'

'Oh no,' she gasped. But she never apologized. 'That's nothing in comparison,' she muttered beneath her breath (referring to the traumatic labour she had just been through).

She was discharged from hospital a day later and was happy to be in her own home with her little angel. Terry and Cheryl decided to name her Treasure, since she was their firstborn, and what a treasure she was.

Terry proved to be a fantastic dad, burping, changing nappies, and giving her baths. Cheryl couldn't have and wouldn't have asked for a better dad for her child.

As the presents and the visitors started to roll in, as Terry was not only from a large family, but he had lots of friends and was very popular amongst his work peers. Cheryl couldn't help but notice that the only visitors that she got were her mother, her dad, and her sister. The relationships between her and other family members were strained, and her friendships had deteriorated beyond repair, or so she thought. Within, Cheryl was hurting, but she was determined that she wasn't going to let her pain be exposed for all to see, especially not during such a beautiful moment.

They continued to play the happy family—Terry the doting dad and the supportive husband, and Cheryl, the wife who was so eager to please.

Chapter 11

Terry had now finished his training to become a doctor and had gotten a post as a consultant in a neighbouring county, thirty-five miles from home. That meant that he had to commute five days a week. Neither of them were happy about the distance, since it meant that if there was an emergency at home, he would have a long distance to travel to get back. However, that concern was lost in the elation and jubilation of Terry becoming a fully-fledged doctor. It also meant that they had climbed further up the financial and social-class ladders.

Cheryl was overjoyed for her husband and could hardly contain her emotions. To celebrate Terry's achievement, Cheryl decided to throw him a surprise party. She invited most of his friends and family and her parents and sister. The party was to be held at the Ritz in London, almost one hundred miles from their home. But she was determined to express how proud she was to be Terry's wife.

The day before the party, Cheryl booked themselves into the Ritz, pretending that she was whisking Terry away for a couple of days. In tow was their little princess; they were no longer a family of two, but a threesome. It was the first time that they had gone away together as a family of three, and to Cheryl this felt weird, knowing they wouldn't be able to explore the town as they used to. However, she wasn't prepared to leave Treasure with anyone, since she hadn't yet and still didn't feel ready to, even after seven months.

Upon their arrival at the hotel, Terry was impressed, since the Ritz was one of the plushest hotels in London.

'This must have cost a fortune,' he expressed.

'Nothing is too costly when it comes to you, darling,' she gushed.

'You must have hammered your credit card.'

'Let's just enjoy ourselves, and if my card hits its limit, then my highly paid consultant of a husband can bail me out,' she said with a proud tone in her voice.

Terry pulled her close and gave her a kiss on the head, liking the prospect of Cheryl being dependent on him.

They walked up to the receptionist. 'Can I help?' a dainty woman, who looked as if she was in her mid-twenties, asked.

'Room for Doctor and Mrs. Odazic!'

Terry looked at Cheryl with amusement. This was the first time she had ever referred to him as a doctor. He saw the pride glowing in his wife's eyes and turned to look at his seven-month-old daughter, strapped to her mother's bosom, who was totally unaware of her daddy's achievement. He fought back tears; it meant so much to him, as a man, to have his wife not only acknowledging his achievements, but to also be so boastful about him.

The receptionist smiled and looked up at them both. 'Doctor of what, may I ask?'

Before Terry could explain, Cheryl blurted out, 'He's a surgeon, and have no fear, whilst he's here.'

They all laughed.

'How old is the little one?' the dainty receptionist asked.

'Seven months,' replied Terry, stretching out his hand to stroke little Treasure's cheek. She responded playfully by kicking her feet.

'Second floor, room number twenty-seven,' said the receptionist as she handed them the keys.

Terry struggled with the suitcases while Cheryl carried Treasure to the lift. They had so much luggage that it seemed Cheryl had packed for a month instead of two nights.

On entering the room, Terry threw himself across the bed and started bouncing on top of it, making sexual gestures. Cheryl gave a big, dirty laugh since she was in the mood to please her husband. While Terry unpacked the suitcases, she gave Treasure her night bath and fed her, with the hopes of getting her settled for bed early, so that she and Terry could spend as much time together as possible before she woke again.

Terry ordered room service from the kitchen. He ordered pork lions, asparagus, and roasted potatoes for himself, along with a bottle of champagne, whilst Cheryl had lasagne. Terry kept feeding Cheryl his asparagus, suggestively pushing his fingers in her mouth. Asparagus was said to be an aphrodisiac, so Terry had ordered them deliberately.

Cheryl began to lick and suck at Terry's fingers after each asparagus. She started panting heavily, and she could feel herself becoming aroused. Terry dipped one of the asparagus in his gravy and allowed it to dribble down Cheryl's neck and onto her bosom. He stood up from his chair, pulled Cheryl's chair toward him, and began to lick her neck. He slid his tongue all the way down her neck and buried his face into her bosom. Cheryl could feel that he was now as hard as a rock. He undid her buttons, and by now, he was burning with desire for his wife. They were trying their best not to wake Treasure, who was sleeping in the cot in the bedroom. Terry pulled Cheryl up from the chair and pinned her against the wall. She undid his trousers and minutes later, they were both lying on the floor, sweat dripping from them both, panting like two dogs who were left without water in sweltering heat.

'Wow, that was mind-blowing,' blurted Terry.

'Not only do I have a brain for a husband, but I've got a stallion as well. I'm a lucky girl.'

They both chuckled.

The following morning, they went for breakfast in the restaurant's dining area. Terry was still oblivious to the party that Cheryl had planned. Whilst they were having breakfast, Cheryl pretended that she was heading for the toilet, but instead met up with the organizers and planners who were arranging the party for her. On the floor above theirs, Cheryl's parents and sister were holed up in two rooms so that they wouldn't be spotted by Terry, which would make him suspicious. To remain hidden, they had their breakfast delivered to their rooms.

In neighbouring hotels, other guests, such as Terry's brothers, his brothers' wife, and his best friend, Naz, had checked in.

Cheryl was pleased with the preparations and sneaked to her parents' and sister's rooms to inform them. There, she quickly exchanged fashion tips with her sister before heading back to the dining area, where Terry and Treasure were. Terry had started to get concerned, since Cheryl had been gone for a while. Little Treasure had filled her nappy and had started to get twitchy. He picked Treasure up and was heading for the lifts when he met Cheryl on the way down. He breathed a sign of relief. 'Did you go all the way to the room to use the toilet?' he asked.

'Yes, it takes a while for my bum to get acquainted with strange toilets, so it prefers to stick to one that it's kissed before,' she said cheerily. He laughed and pinched her bum. 'Were you off to find me?'

'Not really, Treasure has filled her nappy.'

So they abandoned breakfast and returned to their room.

Later that evening, Cheryl convinced Terry to walk to the hotel bar with her for a drink. He was concerned, sure that there would be smokers in the bar, and he didn't want little Treasure to be a passive smoker. However, Cheryl insisted on them having a look around and promised that if they saw anyone smoking, they would return to their room immediately. Terry agreed.

On their way to the bar, Cheryl diverted Terry to a plush hall. Here were the waiting guests and several well-set tables with the most exquisite crockery imaginable.

'Surprise!' everyone shouted as they walked in.

Little Treasure was startled by the noise and started to howl. Cheryl did her best to settle her, whilst Terry looked at the guests in amazement.

'Did you organize this, Cheryl?'

'No, dear, your fairy godmother did,' she responded sarcastically.

He pulled her close to him and gave her a kiss on the lips, and then he kissed Treasure, who had stopped howling and was, at this point, scanning the room with her big brown eyes.

He took Treasure from Cheryl and went off to mingle.

At the end of the party, Terry suggested that Cheryl leave Treasure with her parents for the night, since they were only a floor above them and could return Treasure, if they were struggling with her. He was planning a night of passion.

'Let's see if we can recreate last night.'

The hair on the back of Cheryl's neck stood up at that thought. They ordered two bottles of champagne from the bar and ran a warm bath filled with bath scents and oil.

'Have I ever told you how much I love you, Mrs. Odazic?'

'Show me just how much, Dr. Odazic.'

Within seconds, there were screams of passion coming from their room.

Chapter 12

Twelve months had gone by, and it was time for Cheryl to return to work, her one year of maternity leave was over. Cheryl decided that she wanted a supervisory post and didn't want to return to the job she had held, prior to having Treasure. However, when the subject was approached with Terry, it was met with an instant dismissal. A row ensued, and Cheryl was left flabbergasted. She couldn't understand why he reacted that way, since he had always supported her and encouraged her to aim high. And she was supportive and proud of his accomplishments as a surgeon.

Cheryl decided that she was going to follow her dreams and not be put off by Terry. She started to scan the local papers and searched the internet. She submitted three on-line applications for pharmacy consultants and was invited by two of them to come in for interviews. Cheryl was ecstatic, as the positions were highly competitive, and she knew that they must have been impressed with her CV. Cheryl knew that Terry wasn't happy for her to get any form of promotion in her field, but she thought he might be impressed that she was shortlisted.

On his return from work one evening, Cheryl met him in the hallway as he was taking off his coat.

'Hi, babe. How was your day?'

'I did my first heart bypass today—daunting, but inspiring.'

'Whoooo,' Cheryl gushed.

'And you and Treasure?' he asked.

'We both had a fantastic day. Treasure took her first step, and I've been shortlisted for two pharmacy consultation posts.'

Terry's face became red with anger, and he pushed past his wife, narrowly missing hitting her with his briefcase as he fought to squeeze past her in the hall, which was cluttered with Treasure's pram and toys.

Cheryl was frozen to the spot in disbelief. This was the second time she had ever seen her husband angry, but his anger on this occasion was by far more intense than the first and she couldn't understand why he had reacted in such a hostile manner. She began to retrace in her mind with everything that had occurred since Terry had walked through the door, evaluating and scrutinizing every word that she had just uttered to him. *Did I say something insulting without realizing it? Is he upset because he missed Treasure's first step?* she thought to herself.

She followed Terry upstairs, where she found him looking at Treasure, who was in a deep sleep. She stared at him while he stroked Treasure's tiny little fingers. She didn't know what to feel—she was too numb to be angry, too confused to seek clarification, and too scared to act brave. In the past, Terry had expressed his disapproval of her being promoted, but he had never displayed this anger before, not since they've been married or during the years of their courtship. Not with the incident with the shoe even, as on reflection she now believes that his anger on that day could be justify.

He pretended that he wasn't aware of her presence as he stroked Treasure's fingers. Cheryl left the room in disbelief and retired to bed.

When the numbness wore of, she became inconsolable with grief. She hadn't cried this hard since Treasure's birth, nor had she experienced such pain since then. This was a different form of pain, however, and no amount of pain killer could ease it.

Terry's behaviour was inexcusable, and whilst she was prepared to ignore it until the morning, she wasn't prepared to be the passive wife and accept her husband's rudeness. *Not even with his bloody doctorship*, she thought to herself.

The following morning, whilst Treasure was having her breakfast of apple and oat cereal and a slice of toast, she confronted Terry, who was shaving in the bathroom.

'I found your behaviour last night to be disgraceful,' she fumed.

'My behaviour?' retorted Terry. 'What caring mother leaves her one-year-old baby to return to work? You should be ashamed of yourself,' he shouted back.

By now, Cheryl was close to tears. Here was the father of her child and the man she loved, indirectly accusing her of neglecting her own baby. There were three roles in life that Cheryl took great pride in. One was being a caring daughter to her mother, the other was to being a fantastic mother to Treasure, and the role that she grew into beyond her own expectation, was being a great wife to Terry. She felt as though someone had just ripped her guts out, because she loved Treasure and was completely and utterly dedicated to her. To be accused of not being caring toward her was the worst thing anyone could have said to Cheryl. It hurt even more because it came from Terry. He pushed past her, through the doorway of the bathroom. She dropped to the floor when she heard the front door slam shut.

* * *

On the day of the first interview, Cheryl had arranged for her mother to look after Treasure. She dropped Treasure off at 11.30 in the morning, since her interview was schedule for 12.30 and she wanted to be sure to be on time. During the interview, Cheryl noted that she was under-prepared and stressed, and she struggled to find answers to the panel's questions.

The panel thanked her for coming and informed her that they would make their decision known in two days time. Cheryl left the room feeling like a failure. She knew that her performance was poor, and she felt that she had let herself down because she hadn't done much preparation for the interview. She blamed herself, and she resented Terry for the stress that he had been putting her through. She raced to her car, feeling the tears building up in her eyes. She searched around in her handbag for her keys and struggled to find the sensor on the remote control to open the car, as the tears flooded her face. She threw herself in her car and buried her face in her hands as she wept uncontrollably.

By now, her husband was her biggest enemy; he had turned her into a fraction of the woman she used to be. Gone was the confident, intelligent, and knowledgeable woman, replaced by an emotionally fragile and anxious one who lacked confidence and was losing herself quite rapidly. She drove home at what seemed to be one hundred and ten miles an hour in a zone where the speed limit was seventy. She was engulfed in anger, anger at the man who dared to destroy her dreams.

She contemplated how she could ruin him in return, how she could make him lose his license to practice medicine by fabricating a story so gruesome that the GMC would dismiss him immediately. Suddenly, she remembered Treasure. How could she explain to her that her own mother had destroyed her dad, who was once a very successful man? The thought of Treasure not being able to have the latest toys, designer shoes, and pretty dresses, of not being able to attend an elite school because she was raised in poverty—because her scorned mother had destroyed her dad's future—was too painful to think about. So she banished these thoughts and drove to her mother's to collect her baby.

There, her mother asked her how she had done in the interview. The one person in the world she couldn't lie to was her mom, so she told her the truth, whilst the tears trickled down her face.

Her mom had given up her own career so that she could support her father to achieve his. And whilst she acknowledged that her daughter aspired to be the modern woman who was financially stable and self-sufficient, she felt that Treasure would benefit from having her mother at home to look after her, instead of leaving her with strangers at a nursery, where she couldn't possibly be loved and cared for, like her mother would. She tried explaining this to Cheryl. She emphasized that Cheryl and her sister, who was a midwife, wouldn't have turned out to be so successful and independent if she hadn't spent all that time at home with them.

'So that effort you put in rearing us, Mom, was just a waste. What's the point in raising us to be successful and independent if we're just going to turn out to be housewives?'

'There's a difference between a housewife of your calibre, and one who can barely read.'

'No, Mom, a housewife is a housewife, regardless.' Cheryl packed up Treasure's belongings and headed home. Her heart began to race when she arrived home, as it brought back memories of how her relationship with Terry had deteriorated. She was always open and honest with Terry about everything, and now, here she was, sneaking off to interviews, terrified that he might find out. However, she couldn't help but continue looking at the job bulletins, wondering and dreaming of a promotion.

Chapter 13

This once-peaceful and what seemed like a loving home had turned into a war zone, since upon his return home from work most evenings, Terry would seek a fight with Cheryl in an attempt to discourage her from returning to work.

'Where are you getting all this time to search for jobs when you've got a baby at home to look after?' he fumed one evening when he found Cheryl going through job adverts yet again. 'You're wasting your time.'

This evoked anger in Cheryl, and she responded heatedly. 'No, Terry, I'd like to be more successful than I am at the moment, so that I can help to make provisions for my kids! How's that wasting time?'

This caused Cheryl to be terrible unhappy, and she started to have second thoughts about her marriage. She now realized that Terry wasn't as supportive as she had originally thought and found him to be controlling. As long as he was in control, then the relationship was fine, but as soon as he started to lose control, then the not-so-attractive side to Terry became unveiled.

Cheryl began to question her value as a woman and wondered how she had allowed herself to be overpowered by Terry's control. But the truth of the matter was that he was never abusive to her, physically or emotionally, until now. Well, so she thought, as his control was exercised in a subtle manner, so that he appeared to be a supportive and caring husband.

Cheryl decided to abandon her job search and so returned to her previous job. On the ward where she was the link pharmacist, it was time for a new set of junior doctors to start work, since they rotated from hospital to hospital on a six-month schedule. One afternoon, as Cheryl was scrutinizing the medication cards in order to assess the medications, their frequency, and the dosages that were being prescribed by the doctors, a deep voice from behind said 'hello.'

Cheryl turned around to lock eyes with a handsome young man. 'Hello,' she replied.

'I am Dr. Tony, and I start here today.'

Cheryl was totally smitten; she was captivated by the presence of this man she had just met and so lost for words, she could barely speak. She gave a shy smile. Dr. Tony turned to walk out of the office, and Cheryl followed him with her eyes. She scanned him from head to toes, and her heart started to race. It was only after Dr. Tony had left the office that Cheryl realized she hadn't responded to his introduction.

What an idiot! she said, referring to herself. The thought of how stupid she must have looked to Dr. Tony started flooding her head. 'Idiot! Idiot! Idiot!' she kept repeating.

One of the consultants who worked on the ward walked in. 'Are you okay, Cheryl?' he asked in a perplexed voice. And Cheryl thought it couldn't have gotten worse.

'Yes,' she said, and she began to blush.

'Responding, are you? Maybe you should try taking some of your own medication!' retorted the consultant to Cheryl.

Cheryl didn't respond. She was too embarrassed to.

She left the office in a hurry in an attempt to escape her mortification. As she entered the corridor, approaching her was Tony. Her heart began to race, she could feel her stomach churning, and she suddenly had an urge to use the toilet. Cheryl hadn't experienced this feeling since she had left high school. Then, there had been a boy named Fanny, whom she was in awe of during her time in high school, and she would get all flustered and nervous whenever he was around. Fanny was a very popular boy in high school and received an awful lot of attention from the girls around him. Cheryl wasn't in the popular group and, therefore, was unknown to Fanny. He may have seen her once or twice on the school grounds, but he never acknowledged her presence.

Cheryl quickly composed herself before she approached him. 'We meet again.'

Dr. Tony gave a faint smile in response to her comment and headed for the office. Cheryl rushed to the toilet because she wanted to meet Dr. Tony in the office so that she could prove to him that she wasn't an idiot, as she would be able to redeem herself by showing him what an intelligent human being she was, as she wasn't able to do that earlier.

As she entered the office, she could see Tony sitting at the desk, with the phone to his ear. The consultant who had joked about her having a psychotic episode earlier was still in the office. Cheryl did her best not to look at Tony, trying to disguise her feelings for him. She noticed, out of the corner of her eyes, that Tony had turned to look at her with a lingering stare. She felt pleased, since she was confident about her attire and her physical appearance. For not only was she an intelligent woman, but she was also incredibly beautiful. She was about 5 feet 7 inches tall, had shoulder-length bobbed hair, a slim build, a dark brown complexion, and voluptuous breasts that were so rounded and firm. Tony was a light-skinned French man, with his ancestry from West Africa, and nearly six feet tall. He was unbelievably gorgeous, with locks of curly hair and a backside that rivalled Jennifer Lopez's, which added to his sex appeal.

Tony continued with his phone conversation, and soon it was time for Cheryl to attend the ward round. As she walked out of the office, she noticed that Dr. Tony had turned his head to watch her. She now knew that he felt something for her, but was unsure whether it was lust or love.

Cheryl was unaware that Dr. Tony would be attending the same ward round and was unnerved when he walked in, knowing his presence would affect her performance. He sat two chairs away from her, and as he sat down, their eyes met. They both gave a faint smile.

Dr. Dresby started his introduction. 'This is Tony. He will be with us for the next six months, and this is Cheryl, the link pharmacist to our ward.'

Cheryl greeted Tony as if they had only just met, trying to erase the meeting they had had earlier, which she found too embarrassing. As the ward round went on, Cheryl gradually started to gain her composure, and the more she did, the more confident she became. She even forgot for a moment that Dr. Tony was sitting in the same room with her, until she looked across the room and found him staring at her breast. She was wearing a cream-colored blouse with buttons at the front, and in between each button was a gap that exposed part of her fully rounded breasts, lying asleep in her 32 E bra. If she hadn't been so embarrassed by his stare, her breasts would have woken up, and they, too, would have probably died of embarrassment. She was bothered that he wasn't being subtle in his lusting and so openly stared at her breasts, obvious for all in the room to see.

This didn't deter Cheryl, and she continued to discuss the prescribing dosages of antipsychotic medication. Dr. Dresby had made a recommendation for a particular patient to start taking clozapine. When Dr. Tony proceeded to write this on the patient's drug card, Cheryl interrupted. 'This has to be done on an escalation chart,' she explained. 'And it can be given only after the patient has had a blood test that indicates that his white blood cells are normal.' Dr. Tony looked puzzled, and Dr. Dresby interrupted before Cheryl could engage in one of her teaching sessions.

'Clozapine is one of our last resorts for antipsychotic medications. We use it only after trying two to three other antipsychotics, which turn out to not be effective in treating the patient's psychotic symptoms. However, it can cause neutropenia in some patients, and in order to prevent this, a blood test prior to the patient's commencing this drug is done, and thereafter, a weekly blood test is done for twelve more weeks, and so on, explained Dr. Dresby.

Dr. Tony opened his mouth to speak, but before he could utter a word, Cheryl expressed her disbelief at Dr. Dresby not explaining in detail to his student doctor about the processes and procedures that had to be followed when a patient was on clozapine.

'Not "so on," she said, referring to Dr. Dresby's comment. 'The patient has to take weekly blood tests for the first twelve weeks after commencing clozapine. If they haven't developed any adverse effects during this period, the blood tests are then extended to two weekly for the next six weeks. And if the patient still hasn't exhibited any nasty side effects, the tests are stretched out to monthly,' she explained.

Dr. Tony looked impressed, for not only was this woman who turned his head beautiful, but she was also intelligent and knew how to stand her ground. She wasn't an easy pushover, not even in a world that was dominated by men.

Cheryl was pleased with her performance, and as she glanced over to look at Dr. Tony, she could see he was impressed by her. This reminded her of the early days of her marriage to Terry. He would sometimes just sit and stare at her whilst smiling to himself and would show her off to everyone that they met, because he was proud of her and her accomplishments. He used to brag to his friends about how he had bagged the brain of the century, embedded in the body of a catwalk model.

It was easy for Cheryl to see that Dr. Tony fancied her, and this made her day. No more clarification was needed, and now that Dr. Tony was well-informed, the ward round continued, with Cheryl reviewing the medications that were being prescribed and making corrections when and where necessary.

By now, Dr. Tony had lost his concentration and could focus only on Cheryl's beauty and the fantastic job that she was doing. He was completely smitten by her, and as he undressed her with his eyes, he suddenly took in her wedding band. He was dismayed, since he hadn't noticed the white gold wedding band with the gigantic diamond sitting neatly on top of her ring finger. He buried his face in his hands and kept them there briefly, trying to disguise his sadness at discovering that this woman that he was in awe of was already taken—in a serious way. To be someone's partner was one thing, but to be married was another.

The ward round had now come to a close, and when Cheryl stood up to leave the room, she could feel Dr. Tony's eyes piercing her in her back. As she turned to look at him, he must have noticed how embarrassed she was, and quickly turned his head in the opposite direction to prevent his eyes from meeting hers. Cheryl loved the attention she was getting from Dr. Tony, but wished he were more subtle. She was a very private person who shared her inner thoughts with those closest to her.

Cheryl left the ward to return to her base, buzzing with excitement, for in her moment of despair, there seemed to be a glimmer of hope. She couldn't wait to return to the ward the following day so she could see Dr. Tony. On the way back to the base, she couldn't stop thinking about Dr. Tony and how he had stared at her. She particularly reflected on how he seemed proud of her when she challenged Dr. Dresby in the ward round, because this gave her confirmation that his feelings for her were more than just lust.

Chapter 14

The following day, Cheryl returned to the ward earlier than usual, and she rushed into the office, scanning the room in great anticipation. She wasn't disappointed, for there, in the corner of the office, stood Dr. Tony. When he saw her, his face lit up; she tried to hide the pleasure she got from his reaction. Neither of them spoke to the other, but their body language spoke volumes: him, staring at her with a smile on his face, whilst she tilted her head shyly, playing with her hair.

There was a bin in the office that was used to recycle papers. Cheryl was standing over it, engaged in a conversation with one of the nurses on the ward. Dr. Tony approached and disposed of a Seven-Up bottle that he had just finished.

'Since when is this used as a bin?' she said sarcastically.

'Sorry,' Dr Tony responded, bending over to retrieve the bottle. As he bent over, Cheryl's eyes became fixed on his backside. She was captivated by his rear as much as she was captivated by him. *Surely, he must have been at the head of the queue when God was giving away back-side to men*, she thought. *He was sex on legs*, she thought.

This had broken the ice between them, and they became more comfortable and flirtatious with each other. Cheryl would hang around on the ward after she had finished her sessions, and he would stay a bit later than usual. Dr. Tony worked nine to five, just as Terry did, but some evenings he would still be on the ward at 18.00 hours. However, this occurred only when Cheryl was around. One evening, when it had gone 18.00 hours, Cheryl asked Dr. Tony if he was working overtime.

'You must be making a lot of money, working overtime, Dr. Tony,' she said in a questioning voice.

'What's with the "doctor," Pharmacist Cheryl? Why not call me Tony?' They both laughed.

'Okay,' she quipped. 'You must be making a lot of money, Tony.'

'I wish,' he responded. 'I've got some work to catch up on.' Cheryl knew that whist he was using this opportunity to finish his work, it wasn't the real reason he stayed on after work.

As the weeks went by, Cheryl became more excited about going to work because this gave her an escape from her home life with Terry. Things had gotten progressively worse between them, and the only thing that they had in common at this point was their baby daughter. Seeing Tony helped her forget about her woes for at least eight hours, five days per week.

It was clear that both Cheryl and Tony had feelings for each other. However, he never overstepped the mark, since he was aware of her marital status. Cheryl had grown to love Tony, even though she hardly knew him. She had never believed in love at first sight—until she met him—and now she had to pretend that he was just another doctor on the ward. Well, he was, but she felt differently about him. However, she had to suppress her feelings for him, because she was in a marriage, albeit a disastrous one.

Cheryl had ambivalent feelings because she felt it was morally wrong of her to be married to one man and have such strong feelings for another. She felt as though she was being unfaithful, and the truth was, if Tony were to make a pass at her, she would succumb to his advance. She didn't think she had the strength to resist such a gorgeous man, one who exuded so much sex appeal. She was engulfed by guilt; she felt that her behaviour was bordering on, adultery.

For the next six months, she struggled with her feelings for this junior doctor, as she tried to come to terms with what was immoral and what wasn't. One thing was certain: her unhappiness was a distant memory whenever she was in his presence.

At home, Cheryl decided to move out of their marital home, with Treasure, and move in with her sister because things had gotten so bad between her and Terry. She couldn't afford a mortgage in an affluent neighbourhood on her salary, and refused to apply for rented accommodation because she saw this as taking a step backward. This wasn't an easy decision for her, because it meant that she would have to sacrifice her privacy and her space, since she had to share a three-bedroom house with five other people. *This would be like a tenement yard*, she thought to herself.

The separation also meant that Treasure wouldn't see her dad upon getting up in the mornings. She wouldn't be able to hear those bedtime stories that he read to her just before she retired each night. She wouldn't be able to fall asleep on his chest and sleep there until in the mornings. Or the nights that she was feeling restless or unwell and just needed a cuddle to make her feel secure. Although Terry wasn't the husband that Cheryl wanted, she couldn't fault him as a dad. She knew that living with her sister could be only a temporary solution, since Trinny had a family of her own. And although she knew that her sister loved her, and would do whatever it took for her to be happy, she couldn't stop thinking how inconvenient it must be for her to house the two of them.

Trinny's home wasn't as luxurious as Cheryl's. She lived in a three-bedroom semi-detached, and although her neighbourhood wasn't rough, it was by no means as affluent as the neighbourhood that Cheryl had lived in with her daughter and Terry.

The place became crammed with Cheryl and Treasure taking up occupancy. There was only one bathroom in the house and all seven of them had to share this, which was very inconvenient, as time management became an issue. It was particularly difficult during the weekdays, when Trinny had to get the children ready for school before she, herself, got prepared for work. Cheryl found that she had to wait for everyone to get dressed and leave the house before she could give little Treasure her bath.

This new lifestyle disrupted Treasure's routine, since it meant that every other aspect of Treasure's routine was either later than usual or altered to meet the demands of Cheryl's work schedule. She had to make do with a bottle of milk and fruits for breakfast whilst strapped in her car seat on route to nursery, instead of her usual cereal and toast whilst sitting in her high chair in the comfort of her parents' kitchen. Settling her for the night was the hardest task for Cheryl, because Treasure had gotten accustomed to Terry reading her bedtime stories before she would drop off to sleep. Treasure clearly missed him and would scream her little lungs out at night before falling off. Cheryl made several attempts to make her bedtime stories funny and creative, but little Treasure would just scream over her voice, as if she were protesting.

One night, as Cheryl began to read *A Dragon on the Door Step*, Treasure began to howl. Cheryl tried to become the characters in the story and changed her voice accordingly, but Treasure clearly disapproved. She screamed until she became blue in the face because the persistent crying had reduced the flow of oxygen to her brain. Cheryl began to panic.

'Trinny!' she screamed.

Trinny came rushing in when she detected the fear in Cheryl's voice.

'She's gone blue in the face!' she screamed, pointing at Treasure. Trinny was a midwife and had three kids of her own. She had not only seen her own kids turn blue when they hadn't been able to get their own way, and would throw tantrums, but had also seen them collapse in between fits of anger and floods of tears.

Trinny recalled her second-born throwing himself on the floor and screaming his head off in the supermarket because she had refused to buy him a fireman's hat. It was rather embarrassing, since they had become the centre of attention in the supermarket. She could see one woman looking at her with contempt, as if to say 'You've got a spoiled brat whom you cannot control.'

Trinny's embarrassment had turned into anger, and she had snapped at the woman, 'Have any of your own?' The woman didn't respond. 'Do you?'

At that point, Sam was rolling around on the floor, and his cry had turned into what could be described only as wailing. His cries were long and stretched out, with him not stopping to take any breaths in between. His little nose had lost its colour and had gone pale, and the sound of his cry echoed through the supermarket, bouncing from wall to wall. Her ears were ringing from the sound, and she became dizzy out of sheer confusion. Just when she thought it couldn't possibly have gotten any worse, his face turned pale blue. A loud bang vibrated through the vegetable aisle they were standing in when Sam hit the floor. She had only just qualified as a midwife and had never encountered this with Hannah, her firstborn. She became frozen to the spot, and the only thing that could move was her mouth. When she opened it, she heard herself scream. To this day, she has been clueless about what occurred in between her screaming and Sam regaining his state of consciousness. She remembered finding him soaking wet, with a woman standing over him with an empty bottle. His white T-shirt was dyed orange by the contents of the bottle. Trinny was too shocked to ask any questions and was just grateful that her son was beaming with health. Experience has taught her that a screaming baby who doesn't stop for air, is likely to go blue, and the brain's reaction to this is to switch off in order to rectify the condition.

Trinny's face changed from being fearful to confident, and she left the room in a rush, returning with a wet, cold flannel. Cheryl had cradled Treasure in her arms and was beside herself with grief.

'Here, this should help,' said Trinny as she put the cold wet flannel on Treasure's face.

Treasure gasped for air and shivered when the cold flannel hit her face. She opened her eyes and scanned her mother's and auntie's faces, as if to say 'What have you done?' She clenched her fist so tightly that her knuckles became white, and she started to scream so loudly that you could see her little pink tongue quivering. Cheryl, who was consumed by anxiety and grief, looked at her sister, and they both burst out in peals of laughter. Although she could see Treasure's tonsils, she knew she would be just fine.

Whilst Trinny's home lacked wealth, it was clear to see that it was flourishing with an abundance of love, freedom, and happiness. Donavan worked away from home most of the time, which left Trinny to care for their three children, even though she had a full-time job. But Trinny made it look so easy. She had a close circle of friends who would collect the kids from school on days that Trinny wasn't able to pick them up on time. She frequently had visitors and would throw a barbecue as a means of entertainment. Some weekends, she would leave the kids with Mom and go to the cinema with her girlfriends.

Cheryl slowly started to fit into Trinny's social circle and started to feel like a bird that had learnt to fly. She was going to go on her first girls' night out with Trinny and her friends, and apart from the anxiety she felt at leaving Treasure with her mom, she was delighted about the prospect of not having Terry standing guard over her.

It was the middle of winter, and the temperature had just dropped below freezing. She was dressed in tailored trousers and a white long-sleeved blouse, with her cashmere coat thrown over it. Her sleek, shoulder-length bob glistened in the night's light, and as she felt the cold air brush her cheek, she began to scan the left hands of the women in the queue to see how many of them were married, but without the company of their husbands.

It had been such a long time since Cheryl had been out without Terry, that she had convinced herself that doing so was against the norm. She became lost in her own world, observing and taking note of the women who were standing in the queue a head of her. *One, two; there are six women here with wedding rings on who are accompanied by their husbands.* She paused for thought. She was flabbergasted to have counted fifteen women without a man standing next to them, despite the wedding bands on their fingers.

She was so deep in thought that she hadn't noticed that Trinny was trying to get her attention. 'Anybody home?'

This made Cheryl jump. 'Oh, sorry!'

Trinny became concerned since this was the first time in years that Cheryl was out without Terry, and she wondered if Cheryl was scared. She brushed away a strand of hair that had just blown across Cheryl's mouth. 'Are you okay?' she asked in a solemn voice, as she stretched out her hand to rub her cheek. 'You're thinking about him, aren't you?'

'Just feeling a bit awkward, that's all.'

'Do you want us to go back home?'

'Don't be ridiculous,' she said with reproach. 'I'm looking forward to this. Just imagine, being in Broadmore for a couple of years, and then suddenly ...' Cheryl stopped mid-sentence because she could see the effect this statement was having on Trinny, whose eyes were welling up. 'I'm just fine, Trinny. It will take a while.'

'Let's move up in the queue.'

Trinny was aghast at what Cheryl was about to say. She knew her sister wasn't happy in her marriage, but she had no idea things were so bad that Cheryl would describe her marriage, as being in Broadmore Prison. Broadmore was notorious for incarcerating some of the most vicious prisoners, those who had committed the most heinous of crimes. It suddenly dawned on her that Cheryl hadn't told her the entire truth about her marriage. Her thoughts began to race as she let her imagination take hold of her. She imagined Cheryl been handcuffed in a cupboard somewhere in her house, without food to fill her stomach or water to wet her mouth. She closed her eyes and had a vivid image of her sister being whipped and sodomized. The image was so vivid that it made Trinny jump.

Whilst Cheryl was at her sister's home, Terry would visit on a daily basis, requesting that Cheryl return to the marital home. Gone was the warm welcome that used to greet him when he would visit the Hinchman's home earlier on in his marriage. It was replaced with an icy atmosphere, and looks that pierced his body like a dagger. Terry knew that Cheryl had disclosed their marital problems to her sister, but he was unsure as to how much she had told her. This made him feel uneasy and edgy in her presence.

As he scooped Treasure in his arms one evening on his way from work, he noted that she had a gash just above her right eye. He became immediately concerned and, forgetting where he was for a moment, turned to look at Cheryl with a frown. Immediately, Trinny stood up and stepped in between them, using her body as a barrier, as if to protect her sister from Terry. He became aghast at the notion that Trinny thought that her sister needed protecting from him, and was insinuating that he had been physically attacking Cheryl. He looked at her in desperation, as if to say, 'Please tell me that this isn't the case.'

Cheryl found it difficult to hold his gaze and glanced down at the floor. Trinny had a natural gift for reading people's body language, something that had further developed through her profession as a midwife. From years of observation, she could tell when a patient was in distress, without it being verbalised. She could tell the mothers who would do their bests in rearing their babies, and the ones who would end up on the at-risk register, under the care of social service.

Cheryl's reaction to Terry suggested that there was some form of abuse taking place, but Trinny wasn't entirely sure. This is what stopped her from pouncing on him like a sledge hammer pounding away at a brick. Terry longed for a private moment with his wife—there was so much he wanted to say on his visits, but he always felt that Cheryl's big sister stood guard.

It might have been easy to challenge Trinny about her behaviour if she were a single woman, but not only wasn't she single, she was also married to a man who had a reputation for demolishing men who dared to upset his wife. Donavan had a built that gave him the look of a fitness instructor. He had an upright stance and a fierce stare that made his presence very intimidating. It was rumoured that he had crushed a man's head with his bare hands after he'd insulted his wife in a supermarket, and that he had done a stint in prison for doing so. This was, however, a rumour, since no one ever spoke openly about it.

After several months of staying with her sister, Cheryl felt that Trinny was getting annoyed with her being there, since the house was too small to accommodate so many occupants. She was happy being at Trinny's. Being there had introduced her back into a world that she once knew and loved; she had renewed her friendship with Angel, and had been out shopping with her a few times.

'Just like the old days,' said Angel as she reached out and touched the back of her friend's hand. Cheryl grabbed hold of her fingers and stared into her eyes with a look that said, 'I've really missed you.' She dared not speak because she could feel her tears building up inside, and that would have given away too much detail about her marriage and the man that she married. She still felt a sense of loyalty to Terry, and desperately wanted to protect his image, for in doing so, she was also protecting the one person they both loved more than anything, little Treasure.

Over the next few weeks, she had several meetings with Terry outside of Trinny's home, as they discussed how to move forward. Cheryl missed having the feel of her feet buried in their carpet as she walked through their home; she missed her elegant furniture, which only the very privileged could afford; and she missed their home, which was styled and decorated in a manner that could rival any palace, she used to tell herself.

Terry did love his wife and adored his daughter, but he also loved feeling powerful and relished being needed, since that allowed him to assert authority. Cheryl was a successful woman in her own right, and was incredibly ambitious too. Her drive for independence was spurred on by her own mother's willingness to give up her career to become a mere helper, waiting on her dad hand-and-foot. Cheryl wanted her marriage to work, but not at the cost of her career. She wanted her own identity, not to be known just as Terry's wife. She wanted to be able to walk in a store and make a purchase using her own money, not that of her husband. She wanted to be part of a team, but if the other member of that team should falter, she should be able to throw him a helping hand, not perish because his strength had gone. And more importantly, there was Treasure, who would one day grow up to become a beautiful woman. It was of paramount importance that her little girl learnt what it meant to be a woman, because a woman was more than just standing by her man. She should be able to stand on her own and live life to the fullest, with or without a man.

Cheryl decided to return to their marital home under the premise that Terry would be a changed man. She had a list of changes that she outlined to Terry. She wanted him to be less controlling and allow her to choose her own friends, not have them chosen for her, as he had been doing. She wanted him to be less derogatory about the friends she had chosen. And more importantly, she wanted him to stop interfering in the progression of her career and to be more supportive of her. Terry apprehensively agreed to these requests, and, one month later, Cheryl moved back into their home.

For a while, Terry appeared to have changed. The hostility had subsided, and on the surface, he appeared to be supportive of Cheryl's career path. Things seemed to have returned to normal. However, Cheryl still had mixed emotions about her marriage. She was unable to get Tony out of her mind, and she had somehow convinced herself that they would eventually end up having a relationship, even though she wasn't sure if her feelings were being reciprocated. She knew that Tony felt something for her, something that was beyond lust; however, she wasn't so sure that he felt as strongly about her as she did about him. Nonetheless, she was willing to give her marriage a go in order to ensure that Treasure was raised with her dad. This was of paramount importance to Cheryl, as she was raised in a two-parent family, and although she wasn't particularly close to her dad, she credited him for some of the morals that she was raised with. And after sixty years of marriage, her parents were still together, seemingly happy.

Tony had now been moved to another hospital; he left without even saying good-bye. Cheryl turned up at work one morning, expecting Tony to walk through the office door as he normally did. As she waited patiently for his arrival, she overheard the nurses in the office discussing how difficult it was going to be now that the ward was left without any junior doctors. Dr. Bavvy was sick, and Tony had taken leave and wouldn't be returning after it.

'Tony's gone?' bellowed Cheryl.

'Yes,' replied the nurse.

'Is it six months already?' queried Cheryl.

'No. He's taken annual leave, leading up to his ...'

Before the nurse could finish, Cheryl interrupted with what sounded like anxiety in her voice. 'Where has he gone?' she queried.

The nurses were taken aback by her reaction; she was reacting like a possessive girlfriend who had just discovered that her man had gone off with another woman. They looked at each other with puzzled faces, seeking justification for Cheryl's behaviour. She was behaving so frantically and was so eager to find out Tony's whereabouts, that she hadn't noticed their reaction toward her ... or she just quite simply didn't care.

The man who had helped her to maintain her sanity over the past six months, had just disappeared without saying good-bye. The man who had helped her to escape from her unhappiness and allowed her to dare to dream again, had walked out of her life. She was left heartbroken. How could he? She called him every name possible under the sun.

Although Cheryl and Tony had never acted upon their feelings for each other, she believed that he at least should have had the decency to have said good-bye to her. To find out that he had taken his annual leave, and wouldn't be returning afterward, was disgraceful, she thought. If he didn't miss her, he must at least miss her breasts, she thought. He had certainly stared at them enough.

Cheryl later found out that he was to commence his next placement at a hospital nearby.

'When did he decide to leave?' she asked.

'We found out only two days ago.'

'Well, that's two days more than I …' Cheryl stopped the conversation halfway through. She was now drawing attention to herself, her behaviour going beyond that of a work colleague. Of course, no one at work knew the difficulties that she was encountering in her marriage, so they'd be less than understanding if they found out about her feelings for Tony. She envisioned the gossip mill doing overtime on the ward and spilling over to her base at the pharmacy. *Married pharmacist, mother of one, found shagging a junior doctor in the office; they would exaggerate the story.* As she composed herself, she couldn't help feeling that he had let her down. The days when he would stay late at work were a sign that he had an interest in her, and those lingering stares, especially at her breasts, suggested that he wanted her. She had images of him entering her, and these images were so vivid that they left her wet.

However, Cheryl took some comfort from knowing that Tony was still residing locally. She hoped some day that he'd pick up the phone and call her, for she was never going to be the one to make the first move, not only because was she married, but she also didn't think that it was a woman's place to initiate a relationship. She thought that if she did express her feelings to Tony, then he would view her as being easy. And Cheryl was anything but easy. She had never had an affair before. In fact, Terry was her first love. He taught her everything she knew about love and relationships—the good, the bad, and the ugly. He was her tutor; he had taken her virginity.

Chapter 15

The memories of the day she lost her virginity were still quite vivid. Cheryl and Terry had both gone to the library to study. She had an exam the following week, and Terry had to prepare a presentation on open heart surgery. After being in the library for more than seven hours, they decided to get something to eat, since they were both starving. They pulled up at a McDonald's drive through; Terry had ordered a Big Mac, and Cheryl had a chicken sandwich meal, which was her favourite McDonald's fare.

As they pulled in the car park to eat their meals, Terry looked at Cheryl with lust. He placed his hand on her knee and proceeded to run his hand up her skirt. She turned and looked at him with uncertainty. Cheryl, by nature, was a prude, and losing her virginity in the car park of McDonald's wasn't what she'd ever expected her future husband to request of her. She held onto his hand to stop him from going any further.

'Don't be afraid,' he whispered. 'I won't hurt you.'

'It's not what you're asking me to do that bothers me; it's where you're asking me to do it.'

'I will marry you, Cheryl. You're going to be my wife.'

Cheryl suddenly remembered her dad telling her that 'a man won't buy the cow if he can get the milk for free.'

'Can't we wait until we get married?' she pleaded. She desperately wanted to please Terry, but she was petrified that once he sampled the goods, he might change his mind about marrying her. She was also scared that if she gave herself to him in the car park of McDonald's, he might think of her as being cheap.

Whilst these thoughts were going through Cheryl's head, Terry was earnestly begging. They had been courting for twenty-one months, and they had never gone beyond kissing and groping. Secretly, Terry had always wished he could go all the way. Cheryl was an extremely attractive woman, a woman whom he planned on making his wife, and seeing her on a regular basis, and not being able to have her as his wife, was extremely difficult for him.

An argument between the two ensued. Cheryl was now irritated by Terry's pleas to get into her pants before marriage. She was also disgusted at the thought of him asking her to give herself in such a public place. This she found degrading and disrespectful. She always imagined losing her virginity on the night of her wedding, in a room lit with red candles and with lots of red and white roses strewn about.

'I've been with you for twenty-one months, and never before have I asked you to make love to me, and this is the way you're reacting! You'll never find another man on this earth who's prepared to wait this long. This is a testament of my love and commitment to you!'

Cheryl could detect the frustration in Terry's voice and was taken aback by this, because she was unaware that he felt this way. Cheryl had always thought that Terry would have waited a lifetime for her, if that's what it took. She was now left with a dilemma. She was terrified of losing the man that she loved and planned on marrying, but she felt that giving in to his request, would go totally against her morals. But, in the end, her love for Terry helped her to make a very hard decision.

'Can't we go to the Ibis Hotel, just down the road?' she asked.

Terry's face lit up at this suggestion, and his heart started beating at what felt like four hundred beats per minute. He could feel himself getting an erection at the thought of what was about to happen.

'Oh sure!' Terry replied, trying to hide the excitement he was feeling.

Terry took off at a speed that would have earned him three points on his license on the motorway if caught. When they arrived at the Ibis Hotel, he escorted Cheryl out of the car, and when he took her hand, he could feel it trembling. He felt responsible for the effect all this was having on Cheryl, but nothing was going to prevent him from fulfilling his desire. It had been twenty-one months, six days, three hours, twenty-five minutes, and one second since he last had sex, and he was like a pressure cooker about to explode.

'You will be okay,' he said to Cheryl, trying to reassure her.

She responded with an embarrassed smile.

The receptionist at the desk was a short and slim man who greeted them with a London accent. 'Hello. How can I help?' he asked.

'Not from around here,' Terry stated, trying to make small talk. At least on the surface, that's how it seemed. But whilst Terry was more than happy to explore the body of his wife-to-be, he did not want the world, especially Cheryl's parents, to know that they had done the deed prior to marriage, since this would have tainted his and her reputation. Cheryl's parents were devout Christians who would frown upon sex out of marriage, deeming it fornication. And a fornicator, according to Cheryl's dad, can have no relationship with God.

By ascertaining whether the receptionist was a local, Terry would know whether to be frightened that his secret might be exposed, or feel confident that no one would ever learn of their indiscretion. The receptionist told him that he was from London, but was living in a village close by, and had done so for several months. Terry felt reassured by this because the village mentioned wasn't an area that they were familiar with.

'Room for two?' Terry asked.

'Third floor, room 101,' the receptionist replied.

As the keys were handed over, Terry looked at Cheryl and smiled. Cheryl was unsure whether to smile or cry, having ambiguous feelings. Here she was about to lose her virginity to the man she loved and adored; however she was doing so outside of marriage, and she felt uneasy and petrified.

As they climbed into the lift, Terry took her hands and once more tried to reassure her that she was doing the right thing. The lift door opened, and he stretched his arm out, signalling for Cheryl to exit the lift ahead of him, as he always did. These little tender moments were one of the reasons why Cheryl loved Terry so much. He was by no means a chauvinist, but was a real gentleman. She stepped ahead of him, as he had indicated for her to do, and upon leaving the lift, she took him by his hand and lead the way.

Their room was two doors down the corridor, and when they arrived at the door, Terry could once again feel his heart racing. He could see through the cream, round-neck top that she was wearing that Cheryl's nipples had become erect. He could tell by the look on her face that her anxiety had subsided and she wanted him as badly as he craved her.

As they entered the room, Terry started tearing at Cheryl's clothing, and she, in turn, responded by undoing his zipper. She placed her hand inside his trousers and, for the first time, felt the size of his manhood. It must have been about four inches in girth and nine inches in length. As she grasped it in her hands, she wondered where it would fit. She had never had anything enter her before, and the thought of a part of another human's anatomy, the size of a tractor hose, penetrating her was a daunting one. But she told herself that it had to happen one day, and did her best to get over this hurdle.

Terry was breathless and uttered sounds of passion as he rolled off her. For Cheryl, though, it was an ordeal that she found physically painful. It was not how she'd imagined it. She thought that she, too, would have experienced some form of pleasure. Instead, she was left feeling bruised and sore.

Walking, stooping, and bending her legs for the next couple of days afterward were quite uncomfortable for Cheryl. However, she dare not disclose this to her parents, and so had to mask the discomfort that she was feeling.

Terry seemed to have gotten more protective and loving toward her after this. After all, there were only a few women who, at the age of twenty-four, could proclaim to be virgins, and even fewer could actually prove it. Terry felt he had a precious diamond, and he was going to cherish it.

Several more sexual encounters will follow this night of passion, but not before marriage, she thought. Terry, on the other hand, had a different plan, he had had a taste of the honey, and he wasn't about to leave the honey in the beehive for the bees, without him exploring it. But Cheryl found the guilt and the embarrassment too overpowering, and was adamant, that this encounter would never occurred again, until after their marriage.

Unfortunately, Tony never did get in touch. Years went by, and Cheryl would still think of Tony. She had visions of meeting him and him asking her out on a date. Or even better still, telling her that he loved her. She had revised her response over and over, just to ensure that she would get it right when he did ask. As each day went by without a phone call from Tony, Cheryl became more frustrated. She was frustrated because, she felt that her morals had gotten in the way of what could have potentially brought her happiness.

At work, the promotion to supervisor that she was promised finally came through, and Cheryl was now a senior pharmacist. She shared her news with Terry, who responded with excitement. However, his reaction seemed somewhat forced, and Cheryl wasn't convinced that he was genuinely happy for her. But things had just gotten back to normal, and she didn't want to ruin that. So she didn't challenge Terry about this.

Treasure was now two years old, and she was a real daddy's girl. She would sit by the door, awaiting her dad's return from work every evening, and when his car pulled in the drive, she would shout 'Daddy, Daddy!' She had begun to formulate words and sentences and was a real chatter box. It was difficult for anyone to get a word in once she started to speak.

She liked being the centre of attention, which she so often was. Everyone who came in contact with her adored her. She was a chubby baby, with the deepest dimples in each of her cheeks. She had an ivory complexion, which she got from her dad being a Syrian and her mom being a light-skinned Afro-Caribbean. She had piercing, big eyes that give the impression that she was always excited. Her dark brown hair complemented her red lips. She was an entertainer and loved singing and dancing, and Terry would sit and watch her for hours when she put on a show for him.

But she was a spoilt child who would scream her lungs out if she couldn't get her way. This technique that she had conjured up was effective, especially with her dad. One weekend, as Terry sat down to watch his favourite television programme, *The X Factor*, little Treasure decided that she didn't want to go to bed but, instead, would rather join her dad downstairs while he watched television. Cheryl decided against this since it had gone past 20.00 hours. Treasure started to scream her lungs out, as though she were in training for the opera. But Cheryl ignored her screams. Terry was clearly disturbed by this and came bursting through the door of the bedroom, as though he were being chased by a wild animal.

'You can't let her scream her head off like that!' he ordered as he bent over to pick Treasure from her cot. Treasure immediately became silent when her dad wrapped her in his arms; she placed her head on his shoulders, as if to seek sympathy for her plight.

That night, Treasure didn't return back to bed until it was 22.30 hours, because she would stick her bottom lip out and grimace at the mention of the word 'bed.'

This broke Terry's heart; he hated to see his little princess unhappy, and she knew this only too well. This wasn't a behaviour that was put on display when Cheryl was home alone with Treasure, but when Terry was around, Treasure became a screaming baby. Terry would always succumb to Treasure's screams, and let her have her own way.

She was growing up so fast and was a precocious child. They were both keen for her not to be an only child, so they talked about expanding their family. Nine months later, Cheryl gave birth to Omar. Omar was a carbon copy of Cheryl; he had her rounded nose, her full lips, and her big, piercing, alluring eyes. Cheryl was as ecstatic at his birth as she was when Treasure was born, but once again, his birth reminded her of how lonely she was.

Chapter 16

Although the marriage was progressing well, Terry had ceased his controlling ways; he didn't make a fuss about her working and she could sit and talk with her family on the phone without feeling as though her home had become a battle field. She and Terry had also resume to the warmness and loving nature that they had during the earlier days of their marriage. Cheryl now acknowledged that she needed to broaden her social network, because she needed friends other than Terry. She spoke to Terry about how she would like to rekindle her friendships with her former friends, but he didn't welcome the idea.

'What are you so afraid of?' asked Cheryl.

'Afraid? What do you mean?' Terry responded.

'There are some insecurity issues going on within you, and I am on the receiving end of them.'

Terry didn't respond to Cheryl's accusation. Instead, he digressed. 'We're invited to my sister-in-law's dinner party.'

This left Cheryl seething with rage, since she wanted to discuss a subject that was close to her heart, but Terry had chosen to ignore her.

The growth of the marriage was short-lived because Terry demanded that Cheryl quit her job since her presence was needed more at home than at work. Terry undermined the role Cheryl played outside their home. He became derogatory toward her in a bid to destroy her confidence. The relationship between them started to become strained once more, so Cheryl decided that she was going to get in touch with her old friends. She needed the support, especially now that she had two children, and felt so alone in her marriage. She was concerned about how her friends would react to her, because of some of the awful things that she had said to them, prior to their friendships coming to an end. She had called her friend Macy an old wench who had lost touch with reality, during an argument with her about the lack of freedom Cheryl had since her marriage. She hadn't seen Macy since their fall out, and was eager to re-establish their friendship, because they had had a bond that was closer than that of any of the other friends in their circle. So one weekend, whilst she was sat at home with her kids, Cheryl decided to give Macy a visit.

Macy was a middle class doctor who was also married to a doctor, John. She was twenty five years older than Cheryl and had a wealth of experience in life. Macy had three children, whom Cheryl hadn't seen since their fall out. A lot had happened in Macy's life during Cheryl's absence from it. When she contacted Macy, Cheryl was surprised at the warm welcome that she received from her. But she was even more astounded at Macy's appearance. Since Cheryl had last seen her, Macy had gone grey beyond her years, and her face was creased with wrinkles, with a frown line that was so heavy that she reminded Cheryl of Aunty Susie.

'Are you angry at me for the way I treated you?' asked Cheryl.

'No,' replied Macy. 'I was always looking forward to this day. I knew you'd get back in touch one day.'

'How?' asked Cheryl with a puzzled expression on her face.

'Let's just say life is a learning curve, and I've learnt a lot about relationships, including that of my own. Well, let's not dwell on the past. I bear no grudge. How are you?'

Cheryl burst into tears, partly because she was relieved at how understanding Macy was, and partly because she had so much hurtful and negative news about her marriage to share with Macy.

Surprisingly, Macy didn't seem at all surprised by Cheryl's news. 'I had an inclination that you would get an insight into your marriage; we could see the control that he exerted over you. My concern was that one day it would result in physical abuse. I didn't want you to go down the same path that I have travelled.'

Cheryl was taken aback by Macy's comment, because she had always thought that Macy's marriage was ideal. After all, they were two very educated individuals who were well-respected amongst their peers and their neighbours. John always seemed to be so fond of Macy, and they appeared to be in love.

'What do you mean?' Cheryl asked.

'My marriage has been as colourful as the rainbow. There's been laughter, and there's been sorrow and ...' Macy stopped, and her eyes welled up. She had never exposed her emotions like this before, and she had never disclosed the circumstances of her marriage to anyone. To discuss the issues that were happening was taboo, since she had been taught by her own mother to honour her husband, even if he wasn't an honourable man. But she felt that she had to warn Cheryl about the possible dangers that could befall her and her children, if she didn't take action.

Cheryl sat, wide-eyed, looking at Macy. She was in shock and couldn't believe what Macy had just revealed. On the surface, Macy seemed to have had it all: the husband with the flourishing career; herself, an independent woman; and her three kids, all university-educated. But Cheryl was about to learn more about the sacrifices that Macy had made in keeping the family together, within the white picket fence. With tears streaming down her face, Macy began to tell her story.

'I tried to keep my family together because I thought that would have been better for the kids ... emotionally, socially, and financially.'

Cheryl handed a tissue to Macy, who was overwhelmed with tears.

'The kids had everything that they ever needed, and more. They've all been to private schools, and I couldn't have done that on my own, not even on a consultant's salary. John would beat me in front of the kids, slamming my head against the wall, his fist pounding my cheeks. I had to have plastic surgery on my nose after one of his beatings. But I kept telling myself that I was doing it for the family. The luxurious holidays, the designer outfits … well … if I had the chance to do it all over, I would have done it differently.'

The truth was that Macy's husband had turned out to be a violent man who hid behind his high-profile job and his middle-class status. During the day, he was a competent surgeon who had saved many lives through his skills. His colleagues nicknamed him 'the hand of God', because every operation that he had ever performed, had had a successful ending. He portrayed himself as being the doting dad who cared for and loved his wife. But by night, he was an adulterer who resorted to physical abuse to restrain his wife from challenging his behaviour. This was a well-kept secret, since no one outside of their home knew about the dark side of this middle-class home.

Mary, Macy's eldest, was a general practitioner and had been in and out of psychiatric hospitals since the age of sixteen. She was diagnosed as having a personality disorder, and would often harm herself. Macy attributed this behaviour to the years of watching the abuse she sustained at the hands of her husband, and believed Mary blamed herself for her mom's suffering. Mary had once asked her mother why she stayed in such a violent marriage, she had answered simply 'for you.' Hence, Mary blamed her mom's tolerating the abuse on herself—Mary didn't believe that her mother would have stayed in such a horrendous relationship, if she wasn't trying to make their life as fulfilled as possible. Mary grew up resenting her accomplishments and hating herself, and the only way she knew to ease this pain, was by cutting herself until she bled. Most of these wounds needed stitches.

Macy was in despair over Mary's diagnosis. She, herself, was a consultant on a psychiatric ward and knew that there was no quick fix for treating someone with this diagnosis. There wasn't a formulated plan of care for treating this disorder, and nurses and doctors were oftentimes left exhausted and bewildered from trying to devise an effective plan of care for such a patient. After all, it wasn't an illness that could be treated with medication. How do you treat someone's personality with a tablet? For individuals with such disorders, their coping strategies are normally maladaptive, and therefore needs therapy to help them with their coping strategies.

Macy could see her daughter getting lost in the system, even with her psychiatric connections. She knew that a diagnosis of personality disorder generated negative responses from both nurses and doctors. After all, she was a doctor and had often come across patients with a similar diagnosis, and had been no more sympathetic than her colleagues were being. Macy once had a patient, diagnosed with a personality disorder at the age of twenty-five, who was in her care for six years and who complained that 'the system' had let her down because they had failed to treat her. She had written to Macy in an attempt to convey her frustration.

The stigma that precedes me as a 'PD'

There are several scars that are prominent on both my arms.

They see this as attention seeking.

I'm unable to tolerate people who are critical of me, especially when they're giving opposing views.

They say I'm being manipulative.

I scream, I break things and even occasionally attack the nurse in charge.

This, they call challenging behaviour.

They see the surface of me as a man; they judge me based on what's obvious to the eye.

If only they could see the turmoil in me.

If only they could see the trauma from my past.

If only these nurses would take the time ...

If only they weren't so fearful of what they lack the knowledge to understand.

If only support and coping strategies were as readily available as criticisms are.

Then, and only then, would they begin to understand that I'm a product of my past, from the time of birth straight through to adulthood, I have been punched, kicked ...

Never really had the chance to experience the sound of my own voice ...

Knows not the measures of love and the comfort it brings.

Of course, it's not right to be subjected to the manner in which you treat me, but it's okay because it's how I have been treated throughout my life.

And to expect you to treat me any differently, when schizophrenia and bi-polar is all you've been taught, is inexcusable.

After all, the stigma behind me is more important than I am, as it's more talked about than me as an individual.

So, tell me nurse, what prescription is effective to be given for who I am!

Macy then went on to talk about how academically successful her other daughter, Tracy, had been. Cheryl couldn't help but notice how sad, Macy was as she spoke about the success stories of her children. She should have been bursting with excitement and beaming with pride. But she wasn't. She didn't make eye contact with Cheryl even once, whilst telling her story. Tracy turned out to be a pharmacist, and although she didn't suffer the same fate as her sister in having a mental disorder, she was unable to sustain a relationship. Tracy was on her third marriage, and had had numerous relationships in between these marriages. She'd had five children, two who were born out of wedlock, by five different men.

'Tracy sought the perfect relationship, but there's no such thing. She believes that if a man isn't impeccable, then she's going to end up like me, so she walks away at the slightest sign of trouble. My worry is that she'll never be able to curb this behaviour, and by the time she reaches the age of forty, she'll have forty kids by forty different men,'

Macy said this with a chuckle, yet wiped away a tear. Cheryl was relieved to see that, even in her moments of despair, Macy still had her dry sense of humour.

Cheryl saw herself in Macy, because they had an awful lot in common. They were each an independent woman who had married a powerful man, a man who had turned out to be controlling and abusive. Yet each chose to stay married so that they could make provisions for their kids, provisions that they knew that, they wouldn't be able to make on their own. However, all this seemed so surreal to Cheryl. She couldn't believe that the friend, whom seemed to have such an envious life, had all these hidden dark secrets. This made Cheryl reflect on her own marriage. She knew that just as she thought of Macy, that's how, her work colleagues and neighbours, thought of her marriage with Terry. Like Macy's husband, Terry was a very controlling man, who liked things to be done his way. And whilst she had told her sister and her mom about him not wanting her to form her own friendships, she had deliberately failed to tell them that he sometimes hit her. He had never raised his hands at her in front of the kids, and he had never beaten her to the point where she had to resort to plastic surgery to hide any disfigurement. He was always careful that he never hit her above the neck—he threw his blows on her back, on her thighs, and on her arms. He always avoided hitting her in the stomach, as if he thought that in doing so, he might reduce her chances of bearing him more children. After all, that was what he thought her role as a wife was: to be a baby machine, who was quick to say yes, sir; no, sir.

The thought of Terry hitting her in the presence of their kids made her physically sick, and she started to vomit violently. Macy held her hair back from her face, as the vomit poured from her mouth. She wretched and wretched until there was nothing left in her stomach to be pushed out.

'I'm so sorry to overwhelm you with my gruesome story,' expressed Macy sadly.

Cheryl didn't respond, because she knew that it wasn't just Macy's story that had caused her to have such a reaction, but that it was due as much to her thinking about her own marriage. She knew that it would affect her own children, and she was terrified at the prospect that they could turn out to be like Macy's kids. Cheryl was now gripped by Macy's story, and was intrigued about what happened to her third child, Adam.

'How's Adam?' she asked.

'No, I think you've had enough for one day,' protested Macy.

But Cheryl insisted. 'No, please. I've found all you've told me to be educational.'

Macy looked at her younger friend and saw the desperation in her eyes. She felt a sense of duty toward her. Surely, if my story can be a wake up call to her, then I might be able to prevent her from choosing the same path as I did, she thought.

'Well, Adam, he's doing quite well. He finished medical school and is living with his girlfriend, who's heavily pregnant at the moment. There's no plan for getting married … well, that's what he says, but he's a young man. I'm sure he'll change his mind later.'

Cheryl could see the uncertainty on Macy's face when she uttered these words. She couldn't speak with conviction. After all, this was the same son who had threatened to punch his dad to death, if he witnessed him hitting his mother again.

What Macy had failed to tell Cheryl, was that Adam had turned out to be just like his dad. He had beaten his girlfriend on many occasions, causing her to have several visits to the county's emergency hospital unit. Like herself, his girlfriend had kept her torture from those around her.

With guilt engulfing her face and a tremor in her voice, Macy began to speak. 'Adam and Tracy—so far—haven't been admitted into a psychiatric unit,' said Macy with an expression that suggested she expected them to be. 'Mary's self-harm is due to the years of trauma she suffered from watching me been beaten by her father. And Tracy … well, although she hasn't expressed the reason behind her failed marriages, I'm sure my violent marriage has taken its toll on her. I stayed because I so wanted a better life for them. I thought that it was better to have a two-parent family, even if it was a dysfunctional one, than to have a broken home.'

Cheryl looked on with compassion because she, too, was in the same predicament. She was in a marriage that was far from ideal. She was terribly unhappy, but she kept telling herself that Terry was a fantastic father, and the kids loved and adored him. She had convinced herself that if she wasn't going to be with Tony, then she'd sacrifice her happiness for that of her beloved children, and stay with Terry. However, upon hearing Macy's story, Cheryl wasn't so sure that she had made the right choice. She had never stopped to think that Terry's behaviour could eventually get worse, and that this could have a negative impact on the psychosocial well-being of her kids. She knew she wouldn't be able to forgive herself, if the latter turned out to be true.

Macy's revelation was alarming, but sobering. It gave Cheryl the inspiration that she felt she needed to leave Terry. However, this inspiration was only short-lived, since Cheryl found herself making excuses for Terry. *He's never laid a finger on me in front of the kids; he just wants me to be home so that the kids can have the best upbringing,* she said to herself, trying to convince herself.

She turned to look at Macy out of the corner of her eye, as if she thought she were able to read her thoughts, because deep down, Cheryl knew that she was in denial. She didn't want to face the truth, because admitting it would be accepting that she knew that her marriage had flaws. And although she was unhappy, this was a marriage that she wasn't ready to turn her back on. She had convinced herself that she was doing it for the kids, and whilst that was a fact, it was only a part of it. The truth was, like Macy, Cheryl adored her luxurious lifestyle. She loved the fact that her work colleagues thought that she had a far better life, compared to theirs, and she wasn't going to give them the gratification of knowing that beneath this impeccable image was a family in conflict.

She told Macy that she sympathised with her, but she couldn't understand why she had made the decision to stay, even after the kids had all grown and left home.

'At my age, why get a divorce and be on my own? I'd rather have John, as horrid as he has been to me, than to be alone. However, if I had known that my disastrous marriage would have had such a destructive outcome on my children, I would have left a long time ago. Besides, after Adam became a teenager, John never laid his hands on me again.'

Cheryl thought that Macy had become a needy woman who had lost her self-worth and confidence, and pledged that she would never become like her; after all, she was, by far, a stronger woman, wasn't she?

As time went by, Cheryl's marriage became a boxing ring. Terry would find every excuse in the book to be condescending to her. Cheryl, on the other hand, would retaliate even more by making jibes at him about him being less than the ideal husband. None of this seemed to bother Terry, because he realised that his remarks were having an effect on Cheryl.

By this time, Terry had stop helping with the housework and would arrive home each night after Cheryl had gone to bed. This was a strain on her, trying to keep a balance between her career and looking after her family. Terry was adamant that Cheryl should quit her job as a pharmacist and become a full-time mom, and he knew that if he withdrew his help around the house, then Cheryl would feel pressured and would have to eventually give in to his demands. However, this lack of sympathy from Terry, only made Cheryl more determined to prove that she could do it all.

It was a struggle for her, but she hid this from Terry because she didn't want to give him the satisfaction of seeing her in despair. She demanded to know Terry's whereabouts after work, because he was coming home six hours later than he should. Initially, she thought that he was making himself less present at home in an attempt to leave all the household chores to her, but she began to have suspicions that there was more to his behaviour than just this. She believed that he was having an affair. Not only was he returning from work six hours late, but also, on his days off, he would get up early and take the kids to their usual weekend activities, return them home, and then he left and didn't return until 02.00 hours in the morning. This was driving her to despair because she was afraid of losing Terry.

Chapter 17

The atmosphere at home had become quite hostile, and Cheryl and Terry had regular arguments, which would sometimes result in Terry physically attacking her.

One night, Cheryl was awoken by a key turning in the door, and when she turned to look at the clock, she saw that it had gone past midnight. She threw the bedcovers back and stumbled out of bed, and when she made her way downstairs, she saw Terry throwing his coat over the sofa.

'What time do you call this?' she asked angrily.

'Time to come home to my house,' he said dismissively.

'Oh, it's *my* house now, is it?' she fired back at him.

'I bought it, or have you forgotten?' he replied with a sarcastic grin on his face.

'You patronising bastard!' she barked.

Terry was used to being respected, and hardly anyone ever spoke harshly to him. He wasn't going to accept been called a bastard by his own wife. The veins in his neck became visible, his eyes flashed a look of anger, and he reached out and grabbed her by the arm. He pushed her into the kitchen and shut the door to prevent the sleeping kids from hearing their mother's cry. He slammed her against the wall and hammered her thigh again and again with his heel. The pain rushed through Cheryl's body, causing her muscles to spasm. She screamed and attempted to grab his foot, but she was no match for him physically. He swung her around the room like a rag doll. When the beating was finished, he took her by the hair and pulled her face to his, so she was just inches away from his nose.

'I'm your husband, and you will treat me with respect!' he said with a defiant look.

He was no longer the gentle, tender man whose arms she would melt into when he kissed her. Sex had become a matter of duty rather than two people lusting after each other with such passion, that they could hardly keep their hands off each other. Terry would now demand sex and would get irritated if his sexual demands were not immediately met. Cheryl often gave in to him to keep the peace, but she hated every minute of him breathing on her, touching her, and, even worse, being inside her.

A few days later, Cheryl took time off work after catching a virus that had run through her department at work. As she lay on her sofa in a faint sleep, she felt a presence just inch away from her face. It was Terry, attempting to mount her.

'I want you,' he said and then stuck out his tongue to taste her neck. But he ended up licking the side of the leather sofa that she was lying on, because she had moved in an attempt to get away from him.

'Can't you see I'm sick?' she asked in disgust.

But Terry wasn't listening; he climbed on top of her whilst undoing his trousers. 'You don't have to do anything,' he muttered under his heavy breathing, and he pushed himself inside her.

Cheryl's stomach turned with revulsion. As he thrust himself in and out, with a low deep groan on each thrust, Cheryl was filled with deep resentment for him. She began to scan the room for an object that could be used as a weapon, and to her left, sitting on an oval table, she spied a wooden statue of a man's head. They had brought this back from their Jamaican honeymoon. Cheryl stretched her arm to reach for it. As her fingers wrapped around its rough, elongated form, thoughts of how she was going to attack Terry flooded her mind. *Just hit him in the head, over and over, until his body becomes lifeless*, she thought.

As she lifted the statue, Terry let out a howl as he climaxed. Cheryl froze; she couldn't allow herself to lift the statue any further.

This was a near miss and a wake-up call for Cheryl. She realised how desperate she had become, how far he had pushed her. She immediately thought of Treasure and Omar and what it would be like for them growing up not having a father, with a mother in prison for killing him. She felt her hands shake, then her legs, and eventually her entire body, and she sobbed her heart out.

Cheryl arranged to meet up with her sister one evening after work to explain to her about her marital problems and her plans to leave. But as she watched Trinny's car pulled into the car park at Pizza Hut, she began to have second thoughts about ending her marriage. The thought of having to settle for a less materialistic lifestyle wasn't a thought that she wanted to harbour, let alone experience. She suddenly recalled the conversation she had had with her friend Simone, who had refused to leave her philandering husband, because she knew she wouldn't be able to provide for her kids if she were alone, in the same way she could being married, nor would she be able to afford the affluent lifestyle that she had become so accustomed to. At the time, Cheryl had told Simone that she was embarrassed to be called her friend, because she had so little self-worth.

I'm so sorry, she muttered under her breath.

Cheryl had planned to be honest with Trinny about her marriage, because other than herself and Terry, no one else really knew the truth. But she knew she wouldn't be able to divulge such hideous treatment at the hands of her husband, and still be able to stay in her marriage, as her family would put pressure on her to leave. Her dad was a religious man who believed in the sanctity of marriage and preached against divorce, but even he would turn his back on his righteousness to fight for the happiness and safety of his daughter. Her mom believed that a woman should be submissive to her husband, but if she knew how her child was being treated, she would force her to get a divorce before dying of a wounded heart. And her sister, Trinny, *would kill Terry*, she thought to herself.

'I'm so tired of him telling me to quit my job and stay at home. Sometimes I feel like leaving him, but I'm scared of being alone.'

'But you're already alone,' replied Trinny.

Cheryl seemed aghast at this statement, because although she did feel lonely in the marriage, she didn't realize anyone else was aware of it, nor did she want anyone to be, not even her sister. After all, Terry was still coming home from work, albeit late, but he still was living at home. He still wore his wedding band, and she still wore hers. She was still Mrs. Odazic, the woman who produced two beautiful children for the man whom she once loved and adored. It was difficult for Cheryl to hear her sister speak like that. She knew she was speaking the truth, but she wasn't ready to accept it. So she began to reflect on how happy she was once in her marriage, and how she could go about achieving this happiness again.

'We used to be such a happy couple; I believe we can be happy again.'

Cheryl's sister reminded her that she was never truly happy, since her happiness came with a price. She had once lost all her friends in a bid to keep Terry happy. This made Cheryl start thinking about Tony. Until now, she had never disclosed to anyone her feelings for him. It was a well-kept secret. Cheryl decided to share her secret with her sister. Trinny was her only sister and also a close confidant; she felt she should be able to share her marital woes with her. So she told Trinny about how she was unable to get this doctor out of her head, and how she imagined him to be her ideal and perfect husband. She told her sister how disappointed she was when Tony had left work without saying good-bye.

Trinny didn't want to give her sister false hope, seeing that Cheryl was already devastated over the state of her marriage;

she didn't want her to suffer any more than she already had. She knew that if Cheryl continued to get her hopes up about Tony and her hopes were dashed, as she sensed they would be, then her sister would be badly hurt yet once again. Although she could see that Cheryl had strong feelings for Tony, she also realised that she saw him as the man to take her away from all her problems—a saviour, perhaps. So she made a blunt attempt to discourage her sister from falling into the trap of using one man to help her to escape from another.

'Wake up, Cheryl!' she exclaimed. 'Other than your feelings for Tony, nothing else is real. You have no idea if Tony was ever interested in you, or ever would ever be. And even if he had been, it's been three years since you last saw each other. A lot happens in three years,' she said reproachfully.

Trinny went on to remind Cheryl that she had had two children since she last saw this doctor. 'When he met you, you were pregnant, and now you have two children. There are not a lot of men out there who are prepared to adopt the role of being a father to two kids who aren't theirs. Let's be realistic, you've got quite a bit of a baggage—a husband, two kids, the cats, and that growling dog of yours.'

Cheryl knew her sister was trying to protect her, but that didn't make her words any less hurtful. Cheryl knew that her sister was being brutally honest, but that type of honesty wasn't what she needed right now. However, it helped to put things into perspective for Cheryl. After all, she had far more responsibility now than she had when she met Tony. However, she decided that she would continue to dream about him being her saviour, because during some of her lowest moments in her marriage, having these fantasies of Tony had helped her to get by.

'I'll continue to keep him in my head,' she said with a sad look on her face.

'As long as you know that's where he'll only be,' replied Trinny. 'You don't want to end up seeing him in one of his clinics now, do you?' She said this meaning that when the reality of Tony never being part of Cheryl's life hit home, Cheryl might develop a mental illness, and Tony could end up being her psychiatrist. Cheryl paused for a moment, and then she burst into a fit of laughter, because it seemed so surreal.

Cheryl made a decision, a decision that meant that she might never be happy as long as she was with Terry. However, it would enable her kids to have a secure future, one in which they would never have to do without, and one in which they would never know what poverty was, except as seen on television. And it was a decision that would allow her to continue to live an affluent lifestyle. She decided that she was going to put Terry's happiness first.

Before getting married, Cheryl and Terry had received marriage counselling from Cheryl's dad. During one of these sessions, he expressed that the key to a successful marriage was for each person to put the other person's happiness first. Over the years, this was what Cheryl's mother had done in her marriage to her dad. For the past sixty years, her mother sacrificed her own success and happiness in an effort to please her husband; she gave up a flourishing career in a bid to help him make a success of his. She saw her mother as a weak, dependent woman who was too scared to defend what was rightfully hers, too weak to follow her own dreams. She deserved to have a life of her own, but she instead chose to give up her freedom and became a slave to her husband. Cheryl couldn't help thinking that if her mother had been more assertive in her marriage, then her dad wouldn't have felt that it was his place to give such an advice, as he had done during their marriage counselling. Of course, she and Terry weren't the only married couples to receive this teaching from her dad. There were many others before them, and Cheryl had no doubt that there would be many more after them. *There's no way out for me*, she thought. *My mother has paved the way for me, so this road I must tread.*

Cheryl resented herself for the decision that she was about to make. She was choosing to mirror her parents' marriage, and although she loved her folks very much, she didn't want to follow in her mother's footsteps. Loosing herself to her husband wasn't what she had planned for herself. She didn't think that her place in society was to be carried by a man. She didn't mind being beside her husband, giving him support and being behind him to give him a push when he was unable to cope with life's events, as long as she could retain at least some of who she was. Unlike her mother, she felt that she was a New Age woman, strong and independent and, therefore, shouldn't have to spend her married life trying to appease her husband. She began to resent Tony, and that oh-so-alluring derriere of his. Because if she hadn't met him, maybe she would never have contemplated leaving her husband and, like her mother, might have willingly given up on her dreams for Terry's, before things got to this stage.

She also resented Tony because she some how felt that he should have been able to read her mind and know exactly how she felt about him. She resented her sister because she had the ideal marriage: the husband who worked and didn't mind her being an independent woman with a profession, and who came home from work and helped with the kids and the domestic chores when his job allowed him to. He didn't feel threatened by her social circle, and she could live her life as she so chose. This was the life Cheryl had envisioned as a child growing up. She had always been the stronger of the two sisters. She was the one who stood up to her dad in defiance of his treatment of her mother, when she'd collapsed in front of them from being so tired. She was the one who rebuked him and told him that she wanted to be more than just a wife when he beseeched her to find a man and settle down, just when she had started university. And now, she felt like she and her sister had exchanged their places in society.

Even with all this resentment, Cheryl was adamant that she was going to give her marriage another go, for the third time. She was going to become the wife whom Terry had longed for. So she sat up one night and awaited his return home. Terry was baffled to find Cheryl awake when he got in, because for the past six months, she had always been in bed, asleep.

'You startled me,' said Terry.

'Sorry,' Cheryl replied. 'There's something that I would like to discuss with you.'

Terry began to search Cheryl's face, since he had never seen that look on it before. Her voice was barely above a whisper, and her face looked like a woman who grieved for her child. Terry sat down slowly, searching Cheryl's face for clues.

'You don't have to look so petrified,' she retorted.

Terry didn't respond because he was gripped with anxiety.

Cheryl began to speak; she explained how she was desperate to have the husband whom she married six years ago. She explained how exhausted she was, conducting a marriage that felt like it took place inside a boxing ring. She expressed every word with conviction, but beneath that conviction was a woman scorned.

As time went by, Cheryl fell out of love with Terry, and she resented every aspect of his being and everything that he represented. She continued to say that she would quit her job so that she could be at home to look after him and the kids. At this point, she felt like killing Terry. *The last thing I want to do is to take care of you,* she muttered to herself.

Before her sat a controlling man who had a misconception of what it was to be a man. In Terry's world, a man should be the provider for his household, not only because he wanted to make provisions for his family, but also because he felt that it gave him control of every other aspect of his wife's life. Of course, it was more difficult to be domineering in a household that had a dual income, for an independent woman who was self-reliant was less likely to feel the need to compromise, or toe the line in order to keep a roof over her head, since she was capable of doing that for herself. And Cheryl had learnt by now that for Terry, being a man and a husband, meant that he should be in control of her social circle, the type of clothing she wore, and, more importantly for him, she should be totally dependent on him financially. Cheryl felt that she had lost her autonomy, because being an independent woman was a part of who she was, and it helped to define her. She was losing her status as a woman, now that she was about to become engulfed in her role as a mother, a wife, and a homemaker.

Chapter 18

Terry was ecstatic when Cheryl said she'd quit her job, for he knew that the roles within the home environment would change. He now would be able to be the man that he had always wanted to be. He reached out to give his wife a hug at this long-anticipated news. Cheryl retreated, but immediately composed herself and responded by kissing him on the cheek. Terry immediately asked Cheryl when would she resign and proceeded to give her a hand in drawing up a letter of resignation, not that she couldn't do this by herself—she was an accomplished woman with a masters in pharmacy.

Cheryl immediately got a glimpse of how life as a dependent with Terry would be, but she was determined to play the role of his passive wife. Just five minutes ago, she had thrilled him with the news of her impending role as a wife, so she felt that she couldn't break her promise. One of Cheryl's endearing traits was that she was trustworthy. She never broke a promise. And although she wasn't happy with her new pledge of being the cleaner, the cook, the organiser, the one who'd get up at nights when the kids were having bad dreams, the one who'd take on the role of chauffer—dropping off and picking up the kids from school and swimming, dancing, and karate lessons—she was determined not to go back on her word. So she calmly said yes.

Immediately, Cheryl's resignation was written. It was in Terry's own words, his own typing, his own font style, his own dialect, his own thoughts, and, of course, was done on his own computer. Because when Cheryl decided to give up work, she felt that she lost ownership of everything. She had unwillingly signed her life and everything that came with it over to this man, even her two beautiful children, whom she carried for eighteen months, collectively. She recalled how she had struggled to keep down any food that was brave enough to travel down her oesophagus tube during her pregnancy, which would end up travelling back up the same tube with a speed that would break Usain Bolt's world title. She reflected on how she had had to endure the discomfort of walking down the street as though she was a penguin, waddling from side to side, forgetting what it meant to be dignified, since she would sometime become urine incontinent, not always able to make it to the toilet fast enough before she wet her pants. All this … and now she had little, if any, authority over any future plans for her kids. She was hurt and angry … but was determined that she would adjust to her new role.

The following morning, Cheryl returned to work and handed in her resignation. As she strode along the long, isolated corridors, she stared at the bland wall longingly. She reached out and allowed her hand to run across its smooth surface as she walked. *You've been my therapy, my happy pill*, she thought to herself. The truth was, during these walks back and forth, she was able to forget about her marital problems; she had been able to free herself from all her thoughts and allow her mind to become as bland and as blank as the wall—so peaceful, so quiet, and so free. In her hand, she held her resignation as she tapped on the door of her manager, who was the first to arrive at work on most days. She was an enthusiast who gave her work 100 percent of herself. Katrina had never been married and had no interest in getting married. A Cambridge graduate, Katrina had moved from London to Leicester when this post was made available to her. She wasn't a natural beauty, her nose was too big for her face and her lips … well, she didn't really have any lips, just a mouth.

The news had trickled down to base that Cheryl had handed in her resignation, which took everyone by surprise. It was so immediate and so unexpected, and they all knew just how much she loved her job. She had never expressed to any of her colleagues that she was thinking of leaving. They all knew how determined and focused she had been about being promoted a few months back, and just couldn't comprehend her sudden change of direction.

'Is this really true?' asked Sandy, Cheryl's closest ally at work.

'I'm afraid so,' she replied without looking up.

'What brought this on?' said Sandy as she searched Cheryl's face for a logical explanation. 'You were ecstatic when you were given the supervisory position. You spent the past two years hoping for that post,' she said emphatically.

Cheryl was lost for words. It would have been useless to try to concoct a lie, as stricken as she was with grief.

Cheryl was, by far, one of the most competent, loyal, and compassionate workers within the team. Everyone looked on in astonishment whilst Cheryl struggled to hold back her tears. Cheryl had always boasted about her two major achievements in life, one was producing two beautiful kids, and the other was her job. Now she felt that she had lost them both, and the only achievement she had left was being married—a marriage that she would have walked out of, if it wasn't for the love of her kids. Her own mother had once told her that it was by far more important for the kids to have security by having two parents who lived with them under the same roof, than it was for her own happiness. By now, Cheryl had concluded that the type of dad Terry was to the kids was more important than the type of husband he was to her. Whilst he had failed terribly at being a good husband, he remained a fantastic dad.

Cheryl's contract had stipulated that she needed to give a month's advance notice prior to resigning, so she had to honour her contract, or else she would have broken the legal terms. So for the next four weeks, Cheryl continued to work. She was bombarded with a barrage of questions as her colleagues, some of whom she considered to be friends, struggled to grasp what seemed like a hasty resignation. None of them would have predicted this, and tried in vain to ascertain the truth behind Cheryl's decision. But Cheryl was a very private person who would disclose family issues only to her nearest and dearest, and she put on a pretence of happiness about her resignation.

'My husband is now a consultant,' she emphasised. 'I don't need to work,' she further explained, trying to hide the despair in her voice.

'Is that what marriage does to you?' whispered one of her colleagues under her breath. Over the years, she'd admired Cheryl's passion for her work and her drive to be independent, but now, here she was, proclaiming that she'd be happier being a housewife.

As her leaving date got closer, her guard began to fall as reality became more poignant. For a few days, Cheryl would sob her heart out at work. Sandy had always believed that there was more to Cheryl's resignation than she had disclosed, and believed that her tears were more than just about her leaving work. Sandy had no knowledge about Cheryl's unhappy marriage, since Cheryl had never divulged any of her marital problems to her, and always spoke about Terry as the perfect husband. But she knew by Cheryl's behaviour that something was terribly wrong at home.

She invited Cheryl out for a drink after work, but in her new role as 'the wife that Terry wanted,' Cheryl knew she wouldn't be able to accept this offer, which would infuriate Terry. One of the problems within their marriage was Terry's dislike of Cheryl's friends, since he wanted her to associate with only his selected few. 'I've got some errands to do before I collect the kids from nursery,' she responded to Sandy.

'Then I'll come with you on your errands,' fired back Sandy. Cheryl was taken aback by this, since she wasn't expecting the response. She could tell by her stern look that it wasn't going to be easy to discourage Sandy from coming with her.

'Okay, if you must.' Cheryl didn't have any errands planned; she said this as an excuse for not taking Sandy up on her offer of a drink. But when Sandy insisted, she had to come up with a plan. 'I'll abort my errands for today. Let's go for a quick drink,' she said hastily.

As they headed for Starbucks, Cheryl became nervous, because she knew that she was in for an interrogation, one that she had to be extremely careful about, since Sandy was a woman who had a knack for convincing people to divulge aspects of their lives, that they had no intentions of disclosing.

The cafe was partially empty, and Cheryl led the way to the back of the room to avoid being seen by anyone who knew Terry in case they might inform him, in passing, that they had seen her out with a friend. She knew that this would anger him. She studied the menu in front of her, barely raising her head to acknowledge Sandy. Her behaviour was of concern to Sandy, who could see straight through her and knew Cheryl was trying to avoid engaging in any conversation with her. Sandy knew by her behaviour, that she was hiding something from her.

'Can I take your order?' said the petite, red-headed woman dressed in a green apron and black trouser outfit.

'A cup of black coffee and a bun please,' said Cheryl.

'I'll have the same,' said Sandy, who hadn't glanced at her menu once. She was too busy studying Cheryl in an attempt to see if she could pick up anything from her body language, since she could tell by Cheryl's behaviour, that she wasn't prepared to tell her the truth. And, during the past fifteen minutes, in which they had sat in utter silence, she had picked up a lot from Cheryl. This once vivacious, confident, and talkative woman, who could and would readily engage anyone in a conversation, was edgy, nervous, introverted, and clearly didn't wish to communicate.

'Your resignation came as a surprise,' stated Sandy as she studied Cheryl's face for a reaction.

'It surprised me too, but having two children has helped me to put things into perspective,' retorted Cheryl defiantly.

'Since when has motherhood ever stopped anyone from being a career woman, especially you? You wanted in all, Cheryl, up to even a few months ago,' said Sandy with a sound of irritation to her voice. Sandy was getting annoyed at Cheryl's attempt to try to convince her that being a housewife was what she really wanted. In the past five years, she had come to known Cheryl as a fiercely ambitious woman who would demolish anything or anyone who dared to stand in her way. She would have put off starting a family, until she was at the top of the ladder and was unable to climb any further in her career, if it were left to her willing. She'd frown up on, and criticize every woman who had to rely on her husband for her daily bread. She even resented her own mother for giving up her career at the request of her dad. Now, here she was, about to follow the very path that she had always ridiculed.

'Life is a learning curve, and the older you get, the more knowledge you acquire. I've accepted that I simply just cannot do it all. I'd rather give up my career than to miss out on the valid and quality time I should be spending with my children. I don't want my kids to resent me when they get older, because I spent so many hours working, and not enough being with them. My mom has taught me well, and Trinny and I are so proud of her for the sacrifices that she made in raising us both.'

A lump came to Cheryl's throat at the mention of her mother, at the thought of what she'd gone through with her dad and given up to become a housewife. She had sometimes feel resentment toward her mother's actions, and she had never once thought—until now—that she might have been coerced to do so. *I now understand Mother*, she said to herself.

'Bullshit, Cheryl! And you know it. This is about Terry, isn't it?' she asked with a raised voice. Cheryl lifted her head up and sat forward to meet her friend's stare. Her marriage was an unhappy one. She did feel the back of Terry's hands on occasion, and sometimes even the tip of his boots, and she did question his fidelity, but she wasn't going to sit by and let anyone speak harshly about him.

With her nostrils flaring and her eyes bulging, she snarled at the woman. 'Look, there's a thin line between being a friend and becoming a foe, and I think you've just crossed that line. If you have negative views about my husband, I'd rather you keep them to yourself and not voice them, especially not to me. He is a fine husband and great dad to our kids. How dare you!'

She pushed her chair backward, which made a grating sound on the floor. She grabbed her bag, took out a twenty-pound note, and threw it at the table. 'That's for the bill,' she declared without making eye contact with Sandy.

Sandy followed her to the door with her eyes. Her mouth was wide open, and her jaw was on the floor. She knew Cheryl could get nasty when provoked, but she didn't think that her concerns for her friend warranted such a reaction. *What has he done to her?* she asked herself. Her friend had so much anger inside her, it didn't take much for her to explode. She was fiercely protective of her husband, too fierce, thought Sandy.

As Cheryl approached her car, she began to shake; she was visibly angry, and whilst she was angry at Sandy for the comment she made, her anger was displaced. She got in her car and put the key in the ignition. *Damn you, Terry! Damn you!* She was seething with rage, because everything that Sandy had said back in the cafeteria was true.

She made her way to collect her kids from the nursery, trying her best to put the conversation she had just had with Sandy out of her mind. She had always done her best to protect the children from her problems, and today was no different.

Terry got home at 18.00 hours that evening, as he had been doing since he wrote Cheryl's resignation. The table was set, and his tea was ready, waiting for him, just needing to be reheated. He gave his wife a warm embrace and kissed her on the cheek. The kids were ecstatic to see him, when he used to get home late, they were fast asleep, and he would be gone in the morning before they woke up. Having their dad at home, sitting around the table with them whilst they had their meals, helping to give them their night-time baths, and reading them a bedtime story before tucking them in was like having their Christmas and birthday presents on the same day.

'I'm just going to have a wash,' he said after putting Omar back into his high chair.

'I'll reheat the meal in the meantime.'

Home had now become peaceful, filled with lots of laughter and playtime. Terry would come home straight from work and would be around to help with the kids. Cheryl hadn't been hit by him in the past three weeks, and, in some bizarre way, she felt like she had gained her husband back. But it would never be the same, since Cheryl had given up her job with a heavy heart. She wore a mask at home, at work, and in the streets, so as not to let anyone in her world know of her turmoil and grief.

Chapter 19

It was Cheryl's last day at work, and the manager had organised a little party for her. She'd arranged a buffet-style meal in one of the many rooms that were on the grounds, since Cheryl had objected to a night out on the town. Cheryl felt awkward about the gathering, particularly because she hadn't seen Sandy since they had had their row, and she wasn't sure if she was going to put in an appearance. Sandy always become lukewarm toward her when Terry was around, and had justified her behaviour by saying that she found Terry to be pompous and rude, since he made little or no effort to interact with her when they'd see each other. Sandy and Terry were rarely at the same events, but Sandy's husband was a party animal and would organise an affair to celebrate even the simplest of achievements. His social circle overlapped with Terry's, and it was during one of the impromptu parties that Terry had met Sandy.

Cheryl had planned to keep her distance from Terry whilst at her leaving do, sensing that his presence might get in the way of her bonding with Sandy. In her heart, she wanted to reconcile with her, since tonight might be the last time she would have the opportunity to see her face-to-face; once she was back home with Terry, she expected him to set restrictions as to whom she could and couldn't speak to.

When she walked into the room, she was surprised to see the effort her colleagues had gone through for her. There was a chocolate fountain in the far corner, because they knew she was a great lover of chocolate. A bar was set up on the right side of the room; she spotted a fridge packed with bottles of champagne and other beverages, and nudged Terry in his side.

'They made preparation for you, then,' she said teasingly.

There must have been at least twelve different dishes, ranging from Chinese to Indian to Italian to Caribbean, laid out around the room for self-service.

'This is what you'd call a multicultural dinner,' she said with a giggle.

Her work colleagues were of a variety of ethnicities and races, and it seemed that efforts were made to ensure that they all felt a part of Cheryl's leaving do. The tables that were put out for the guests were far more posh than any she had seen on the premises.

'This must have cost a fortune,' she said in a whisper to Terry, standing next to her.

'I'm heading for the bar,' said Terry as he kissed her on the cheek.

As Cheryl began to scan the crowd to see who had turned out, she made eye contact with Sandy, who was looking at her with an expression that she found hard to read. Cheryl wanted so much to be able to run over and hold her friend, and tell her that she was right about her not really wanting to give up her job, but she couldn't. For in doing so, she would be giving her an insight into the man she had married. And she wasn't prepared to drop the pretence; she had carried on for the past six years about how wonderful her life was with Terry. But she couldn't just pretend that she hadn't seen her friend because she cared about her deeply, and she thought that Sandy's concerns for her were genuine and not meant to be malicious. She had been like a sister to her on many levels, and they'd shared some dark moments too. But unlike the other dark moments, Cheryl didn't wish to bear her soul regarding this closely guarded secret. She plucked up the courage and headed toward Sandy, all the while studying her face to see if she still regarded her as a friend, or if she had indeed become her foe, per Cheryl's prior comment.

'I've been searching for you,' said a voice as she grabbed Cheryl by the hand, distracting her from Sandy. Cheryl turned her head in the direction of the voice to see a set of glistening white teeth smiling at her.

'You've done a fantastic job!' bellowed Cheryl as she reached out and embraced the woman.

'You've been a fantastic employee!' responded the woman. It was none other than Cheryl's boss, Katrina. She had spent the past four weeks trying to persuade Cheryl to rethink her position because in losing Cheryl, she was losing one of her—if not the very—best employees.

'I will be so sad to see you go, Cheryl. You'll be missed,' she exclaimed, trying to hold back the tears. In the five years that she had known Cheryl, their relationship had grown beyond that of just being an employee and boss. They'd shared many jokes together; they'd even gossiped about their other colleagues. It was Katrina who had promised Cheryl a promotion before she married Terry, spotting the potential in her, even as a newly qualified pharmacist. Katrina could separate the roses from the thorn even before she sat down to ask her first question during an interview. She could also tell which staff members would be a walking *British National Formulary*—those who would be able to recite every medication and its frequency and dosages by heart, but who lacked interpersonal skills and would falter and fail when thrown into a ward setting.

The day she'd interviewed Cheryl, she knew that this young girl would make a difference in the lives of those who had the pleasure to meet her, work with her, and sit with her. She knew that in a matter of months, she'd be looking to be promoted, since she not only had intelligence, empathy, and passion for her job, but she also had an in-depth knowledge and awareness of her position that transcended her years. If she hadn't been confident about her own role as manager, and believed in her innate skills, she would have felt threatened by Cheryl, for she reminded her of a younger version of herself, and she knew that she'd be able to introduce and bring about changes to her team. And she did. It was Cheryl's idea to institute weekly teaching sessions, wherein she could meet patients face-to-face, providing them with knowledge about their medications, which enabled them to make more informed choices about their prescription drugs.

And it was Katrina who had fought for her to eventually get the promotion. The chief executive had intended to transfer a supervisor from another pharmacy in the region to be the supervisor at Cheryl's base when the post was created, but Katrina had insisted that Cheryl was the best person for the job, and she could be trusted implicitly. He wasn't convinced, since Cheryl hadn't been qualified for very long.

'She's a baby to the job,' the chief executive had stated. 'This man has sixteen years of experience behind him.'

'With sixteen years of experience, Cheryl will be looking to take your position, not to be a supervisor,' Katrina had explained.

'There'll always be a post here for you as long as I'm manager here,' she went on.

Cheryl knew that wasn't likely to happen, unless God came from heaven to earth and gave her husband a new heart.

'I'll hold you to your words,' she rejoined.

Sandy was nowhere to be seen as Cheryl made her way through the room, which was packed with her co-workers. Cheryl began to panic; she'd hate it if the last words she ever spoke to Sandy were the ones she hurled at her on that dreadful day. She pushed and forced herself through little tiny pockets of gaps that were left between those gathering to gossip and drink. She scanned the room, but to no avail.

The patio door to the garden was open, but it was pitch black, and no one would dare to stand out there in this darkness, unless he was desperate for nicotine. As she turned to make her way back into the hall, she heard moaning sounds coming from the darkness. At first she thought it might be an animal, but then one of the sounds was all too familiar. Cheryl made her way to the garden, taking due care not to be heard. As she approached, she saw two figures—one was a man standing, looking down. She was aghast. She gasped for air, her heart raced, and her stomach churned as she followed where his eyes were looking. He had a fistful of a woman's hair grasped in the palm of his hands, and he was thrusting himself back and forth in her mouth, delirious with pleasure. Cheryl became nauseous; she felt her food coming up from her guts, and she held her mouth to prevent herself from throwing up, because she didn't want to be discovered.

'Oh, Sandy, that was bloody marvellous!' expressed the man between breaks of panting.

'Your milk is all over my dress, Terry. I can't go back to the party like this,' the woman whined.

Cheryl didn't move. She stood watching her friend and her husband as they made attempts to straighten their clothing. Cheryl's mind went blank, and her heart was in pieces; she felt numb as she watched Terry and Sandy make their way back to the hall, doing their best not to raise any suspicions. He went ahead first, and then minutes later, she used the side entrance to enter the hall.

Cheryl thought to herself, this entire attempt to stop me from working was a ploy just to keep me from finding out his dirty little secret, and her interrogation was to see how much damage she has done to my marriage, she muttered.

Cheryl bawled her eyes out; she held her stomach, as if she were a woman in labour, and howled. She knew she couldn't go back to the party because she looked a mess, so she made her way through the darkness, taking the long path back to the car park.

She collapsed in her car and wept. She attempted to drive home, but was unable to see the road clearly because her eyes were so swollen from crying. The last thing she wanted to do was to alert anyone to her plight, but she was desperate. She searched her bag for her mobile and dialled Trinny's number.

Trinny arrived in her nurse's uniform in a state of anxiety. On seeing her sister, she thought she must have been mugged because her eyes were puffy, red, and swollen.

'Who did this to you?' she screamed.

Cheryl was unable to respond, since seeing Trinny made her cry even harder.

'Talk to me! Cheryl, please!' she begged her sister. 'Where's Terry? Shall I go and get him?' she asked desperately.

Cheryl could motion to her sister only by shaking her head.

Trinny held Cheryl, who seemed so weak and weary, around the waist and supported her as they walked through the front door. When they arrived in the sitting area, Cheryl collapsed on the floor, knocking Trinny off balance and causing her to fall on top of her. As she attempted to rise from the floor, she looked her sister up and down for any evidence that would indicate that she had been raped or molested in some way.

'I'm calling the police,' she said to Cheryl authoritatively.

'No,' she muttered softly. She held out her hand and reached for her sister's hands. 'Oh Trinny,' she cried.

Trinny was beside herself with worry. 'Please, Cheryl. Please, tell me what's wrong.'

As Cheryl tried to compose herself, she explained what she had seen.

'I'll kill him,' snarled Trinny as she rose to her feet, as if to go after Terry. Cheryl pulled her back and begged her not to.

Meanwhile, back at the party, Terry was searching the room for Cheryl. He had, by now, alerted everyone of his wife's disappearance, and they all acknowledged that they hadn't seen her for a while. He made his way back to the patio door that led to the garden, but he stopped immediately because he had a bizarre feeling, as if he could sense that Cheryl had been there. He rushed out into the inky blackness of the night, and began to search as much as his eyes would allow him to do, in the dark. He suddenly had flashbacks of being with Sandy and imagined Cheryl standing there, watching them both. He buried his head in his hands because the thought was too much to take in. With his eyes clenched shut, not wanting to look at the very spot where he had just carried out his adulterous act, he turned to make his way back into the room.

He stepped on something, something that made a crackling sound. He didn't ignore it because he was hoping to find something that would give him a clue to say that his wife had been a witness to his act. As he bent over and began to search under his feet, he felt a hard object; it wasn't big enough to stand out from all the other clutter and stones that were lying beneath his foot, but it was shiny enough to make him want to have a good look. He headed for the patio, where it was lit well enough to see an ant if one attempted to crawl across the floor. He held up the shiny object, and his nightmare turned to reality. His mouth fell open; he used his free hand to wipe his face in disbelief. Because whilst he'd hoped to solve the mystery of his wife's disappearance, he hoped that she wouldn't have knowledge about what he had been doing—on her night—with a woman—her friend.

There was no mistaking that the diamond earring that he held in his hand was Cheryl's, since he was the one who had bought it as a gift for her when their son Omar was born. He had seen the earring in Dubai when he and Cheryl had travelled there during one of their holidays. She had loved the jewellery and lingered over it; Terry could see how much she desired the beautiful jewellery and had purchased it without her knowing. He had planned to give it to her on her twenty-ninth birthday, but changed his mind and gave it to her when Omar was born because he knew it would hold more meaning to her then.

Cheryl had been totally bowled over on receiving the earring, since she could remember standing in the jewellers in Dubai, looking at this remarkable earring that was so rare and unlike anything she had ever seen before. They later discovered that it was a one-off piece. She remembered how she wished she was wealthy enough, so that she could have ten thousand pounds, as this was the cost of the earring. She had wept uncontrollably on receiving the piece of jewellery from Terry because, to her, this was a confirmation that although her marriage had gone through a rocky patch, her husband did still love her.

Now, Terry sat down on a wooden chair that was on the patio because if he hadn't, he would have simply fallen to the ground. His legs were visibly shaking beneath him, and he felt physically sick. *How could I do this to you?* he muttered to himself. He had had a reputation for being a womaniser prior to meeting and marrying Cheryl, but he'd changed—he'd changed for her. He had never once cheated on her ... until he met Sandy. He would meet up with Sandy after work most evenings before returning home.

Sandy wasn't what someone would describe as a beauty, not like Cheryl. She was okay-looking and had the body of a model, but was not as impressive as Cheryl. But she could give something that Cheryl couldn't and Terry desired. Sandy knew how to give a good blow job. He called her his 'blow job girl.' He had never had intercourse with her, and he had never so much as kissed her. He didn't even fancy her because she wasn't really his type. She wasn't pretty enough and didn't like stylish clothes. And she was rather domineering, a feature Terry found unattractive. But the feeling of having his dick at the back of her throat was mind-blowing.

Two years ago, a friend of a friend had invited him to a party. They'd informed him that the host was a small-business man who liked to consider himself as a bit of an entrepreneur, and relished mixing with people of Terry's kind. Terry took up the invitation after he was told the event would have enough alcohol to supply a brewery for a month.

'This is Antwuan, the host,' exclaimed the friend.

'Nice meeting you. This is my wife,' said Antwuan, pointing to a model-like figure standing next to him. Terry had given the man's wife a double take, not because he found her to be attractive, but because she and Antwuan were so opposite in looks. Terry later joked that he never understood how ugly men like Antwuan more often than not ended up with women who were far better looking than themselves.

Antwuan was a tall man, towering over everyone who was less than six feet tall. But that was his only endearing feature, as he was built like a model. His lips were far too big for his face.

'In fact, I've never known a white man to have a mouth that big,' Terry had giggled. 'You'd think that he robbed an African and left the poor bloke without lips.'

His eyes were so small that they looked screwed up, and his nose was so long that it could have been a Toucan's beak. And next to him stood this tall, svelte creature whom he had introduced as his wife.

Sandy was smitten by Terry on meeting him. Her eyes lit up, and she had a smile on her face that went from one ear to the next. Terry had noticed the instant attraction, and although he wasn't particularly interested in her, the thought of having a one-night stand with the ugly hostess's wife, at his party, was too tempting. Later on that evening, Terry slipped away with Sandy to the ladies' toilet. He was later spotted coming out with his zipper unzipped and a smug look on his face. On his way to meet up with his friend, he winked to Antwuan as if to say 'I've just had your wife,' and Antwuan had winked back, totally oblivious.

'Poor sod,' muttered Terry to his friend, referring to Antwuan.

'You disgust me,' his friend retorted. 'No respect for the man or his wife.'

'I did her a favour,' said Terry with sheer sarcasm.

During those intervening two years, Sandy and Terry would occasionally meet up to re-create that same scene. It was always Sandy who did the chasing, and Terry was always too happy to oblige. The truth was, he saw Sandy as a cheap tart who would fall to her knees any time and any place to please him. Their meetings were always easy, tawdry, quick, and predictable, and quite pleasing for Terry. They'd do it in the car, in public toilets, and in dark lay-bys. He relished getting his thrill in these risky situations, and she loved pleasing him.

It was the middle of winter, and the weather forecast had predicted heavy snow that could possibly bring Britain to a halt. It was three months to the date that she had met Terry, and wanted to celebrate their time together. On hearing this, Sandy decided to leave work early. Her excuse was that she wanted to collect her kids before the treacherous weather took over the country. But instead of collecting her kids from school, she asked her mother to do the school run, whilst she made her way to Birmingham to see Terry. The thought of not being able to see him and grasp him between her hands, whilst he succumbed to her in pleasure, was too unbearable for Sandy. For her, it was more than just oral sex; she was besotted with Terry, and she hoped that one day he would not only take their sexual acts to a different level, but that he would also leave his wife for her.

As he approached his car, he could see her standing next to his ML 360 Mercedes Benz. He was baffled as to why she was there, since they hadn't arranged to meet up, and he was not too pleased to have her there because today, of all days, the last person he wanted to see was Sandy, because he was in a rush to get home to his family before the snow fell.

'Have you lost your way?' he asked indignantly.

She could tell by the tone of his voice that he was less than impressed. 'I've come to escort you home,' she said in a whisper, searching his face to see his reaction.

Terry could be a harsh man when angry; he had the ability to reduce a grown man to tears with words alone. And Sandy knew this only too well, having been on the receiving end of his rages on many occasions. She had become a leash to him, wanting him, needing him, begging him to meet her at the most inconvenient of times. Terry preferred her to stay in the shadows until he had a need for her, but her love for him wouldn't allow her to do this. She was like a woman possessed, with a raging jealousy. She had a grudge against Cheryl, because the man that she desired, loved only her, and she knew he wouldn't give up his family easily, and especially not for her.

Terry had made his way past her since he didn't wish to engage her any further, but she ran past him and stood in front of the driver's door, obstructing his path.

'I'll make it worth your while,' she said whilst fondling the front of his trousers.

'Where is your car?' he retorted.

'I caught the train,' she said.

'Get in the car,' he said, motioning toward her in despair. As he drove at eighty miles an hour down the M1, Sandy reached for his zipper, despite the madness that was occurring on the motorway—cars dashing by at a hundred miles an hour, cars overtaking each other at close range, and one man who was swinging his Range Rover from left to right, as he fought to fit in between cars.

Terry was fighting the urge not to scream as he came, and some of his bodily fluid hit the windscreen. It wasn't the fluid that came from him during an orgasm that made his car sway from his lane into the opposite one, but the spasm that overtook his body and made it jerk as though he was having a seizure.

Chapter 20

He arrived home to find Cheryl being comforted by Trinny. If it hadn't been for her not wanting to add more anguish to her sister's sorrow, Trinny would have pounced on him as soon as he walked through the door.

Cheryl buried her face in her sister's lap and wept uncontrollably at his presence. She wept like a mother who mourned her child. Trinny tried desperately to ease her pain, all the while giving Terry a look that said 'you've done this.'

He looked on and was devastated by the sight of his wife; he was consumed by guilt, and he knew there was nothing that he could do or said that would take her pain away. With his head bowed, he went past the women and made his way upstairs. He wanted to explain, but what would he say, how could he justify his behaviour. He wanted to call his brother, but he knew even he would hate him for what he'd done to Cheryl. Cheryl was loved and respected by his family; they saw her as the innocent girl who had saved him from a life that potentially could have been destructive if he hadn't met her. She was loyal, trustworthy, and committed, and she had borne him two beautiful children. How could he be so callous toward her?

He couldn't stand to hear the sound of her crying. It was all too painful for him, so he left through the back door, and, without any plans, and his mind still blank, he drove and drove. He must have driven about fifteen miles before he started to become aware of his surroundings. To his right, he saw a few houses, one of which was well-lit. As he gazed at the house, he imagined a family living there—a man and his wife and their kids, and he imagined them sitting in front of the TV, watching their favourite programmes. His wife would be lying across his chest while he tousled her hair, and his kids would be sitting at his feet, with everyone engaged in conversation. It brought back memories of his own family, because even though they'd had a difficult patch, they'd also had a home filled with tender and loving moments. But this was now just a memory, one he might never have the privilege to share or create again with Cheryl and the kids, he thought to himself. *Nor do I have the right*, he muttered quietly.

Looking to his left, he saw that he was surrounded by darkness; there were no streetlights, no houses with lights, and he couldn't see more than a few metres ahead of him. Then suddenly, he saw a sign for a place that he was familiar with, one where he had brought Cheryl many times, its acres of green fields and high mountains giving her a feeling of being in the Caribbean. During the summer, it was packed with old and young lovers alike who strode through the fields, holding hands. There were couples with children too, as the site was a magnet for ice cream vans and other refreshment vendors. It was a sight that also attracted tourists who wanted to go hiking and bicycle riding. Yet with all these visitors, it was still possible to find a private spot to escape and take in the fresh air and beautiful greenery.

As Terry turned his car to enter the gates of Bradgate Park, he could hear Cheryl's crying ringing in his ear. It all seemed so surreal to him, and Terry stepped on his accelerator in an attempt to evade her voice. In the pitch blackness of the night, his car hit a tree. A loud bang and then a long screeching sound could be heard as the car made its way for the heavens. As the car returned to the ground, it made a dull thud that shook the grounds of Bradgate Park like an earthquake. Within minutes, Bradgate Park was alight with orange flames. Little hairy creatures dashed across the park, heading for safety.

A man passing by rushed to the driver's side of the car and attempted to open the door, but it was locked. People started appearing out of the middle of nowhere. It was like watching the Michael Jackson *Thriller* video: one minute the park was empty, and within seconds, a crowd had congregated.

'There's someone in the car!' shouted the man, with terror in his voice. 'The door is jammed shut! I need a hammer or something hard!'

Terry's body was dragged out of his Mercedes, and he appeared to be lifeless when he was rolled on the grass in an attempt to put out any fire that was on him.

'Can you hear me, sir?' shouted a man who had come to help. He had been either in the midst of urinating in the fields or he was in the height of passion when the car crashed, evidenced by his manhood hanging from his unzipped trousers.

The ambulance arrived just before the fire brigade pulled in, and then the police cars followed. By now, the flashing red and blue lights of emergency services had added to the lighting of this pitch black park. It was like watching the fire rockets set off on New Year's Day in Australia. It would have been breathtaking if such a horrific tragedy hadn't taken place.

The paramedics gathered around Terry, their green uniforms clashing with the greenery of the park. One man, holding a small flashlight that looked like a pen, was shining the light in Terry's eyes. Another man placed his index and his middle fingers under Terry's wrist to take his pulse. They then placed an oxygen mask over his face before carefully putting a neck brace around his neck. The crowd collectively made a sound that indicated that a burden had just been lifted from their shoulders. This was a good sign, and although the victim was still unresponsive, it clearly indicated that he was still alive.

The two fire brigades, with their eight burly workers, didn't struggle in putting out the flames from the car. The men were tall and appeared to be strong, firmly aiming the hose, with the gush of water bursting out of it, onto the burning car. Their yellow uniforms accentuated their broad shoulders and made them appear to be much larger than they were. The area was cordoned off by policemen, who went around to all the spectators, collecting from them personal details, such as contact numbers and names for further investigation.

It was evident that Terry had sustained second-degree burns on his back, but it was not known what other injuries he had suffered, and there were no open wounds to give any indication. However, through closer examination, doctors noted that he had swelling and tenderness at the back of his head. A CT scan later revealed that he'd sustained a closed skull fracture. Further tests were needed to assess the severity of the fracture to Terry's cranium, and the doctor requested a Magnetic Resonance Imaging (MRI) to rule out the possibility of internal bleeding or leakage of cerebrospinal fluid.

'He's a very lucky man,' said the doctor. Terry's injury wasn't in line with the severity of the accident. His injuries could have, and should have, been worse. The car was a total write off; the windscreen, passenger windows, and the window at the back of the cars were all reduced to pieces. The bonnet of the car had completely disengaged from the car, and the roof had collapsed onto what was left of the seats. The only part of the car left unscathed was the driver's side of it. It was as though an angel had been protecting Terry. The window on the driver's side of the car was left without a scratch; the roof had concaved, leaving the driver's seat and window untouched. The doctors were baffled because, Terry should have sustained more serious injuries—or even death. Yet here he was, with only second-degree burns on less than 5 percent of his back, and his head injury wasn't life-threatening, nor did it need much medical intervention for his recovery.

'His prognosis looks very good,' reported the doctor.

Back at home, Cheryl was still wallowing in her grief. She felt even worse because Terry hadn't returned home, and no one knew of his whereabouts. Her first thought was that he had discovered that she had found out about him and Sandy and he had gone off with her to some secret location to carry on with their filth. But she had rung Sandy's home number, pretending to be a friend, and when Sandy had taken the receiver for the call, she'd hung up with relief, but that didn't lessen her pain. Her thoughts began to run away with her, and she now began to wonder how many more women Terry had been seeing. She had images in her head of the acts he would have these women do for him, or that he did for them, and the thought made her heave. If she hadn't been distracted by the doorbell, she probably would have vomited out of disgust, as she relived the moment she found Sandy kneeling before her husband, with him in her mouth.

It was Terry's brother Sullivan at the door. He looked rather worried, but she thought that he had gotten news about his brother's infidelity and had come around to express his sympathy.

'I wanted to get here before they informed you,' said Sullivan. He thought that the redness and swelling of her eyes was because she'd been informed by the hospital of Terry's plight.

'Before who tells me what?' questioned Cheryl, confused.

'The hospital,' he responded.

She could tell by the despair in his voice that something terrible had happened. Her thoughts went back to Terry, and for a moment she thought that he had tried killing himself. This made her grimace, as if she was feeling physical pain.

'It's Terry, isn't it?' she asked fearfully.

'Why else would you be crying?' asked Sullivan suspiciously.

'What's happened to Terry?' she questioned hastily.

Sullivan was perplexed and suspected that something had occurred between his sister-in-law and his brother. *This may have even contributed to his accident*, he thought to himself.

'He's at the accident and emergency unit at the Royal Hospital,' he explained. 'I thought you already knew that from …'

Cheryl interrupted before he could finish. 'Oh my God!' she screamed, and she rushed off to see to Omar, who was awoken by the raised voices and was now screaming his head off. Cheryl came back running, with Omar, Treasure, and a packed bag. 'I'll have to drop them off at my mom's,' she said emphatically.

The two adults sat quietly in the car on the ride. Cheryl changed Omar's nappy, trying to hide her anguish. Treasure had noticed that her mother's eyes were swollen and red and asked her why she had been crying. She was now five years old and was very observant and inquisitive. She was also a bright little girl. Her school teacher had described her as being astute.

'I'm just missing my friends at work,' Cheryl tried to explain. 'But whilst I'm sad because I'm leaving work and won't be able to see my friends, I'm happy that I'll be able to spend more time with you and Omar,' she added.

Prior to handing in her resignation, Cheryl and Terry had sat their two children down and tried to explain to them the changes that were about to happen within their household. They understood that Mommy would not only be dropping them off and picking them up from school and nursery, but that she'd also be at home with them for the remainder of the day. This had excited them, especially Omar, who was a real mommy's boy.

'Does that mean I won't be picked up by Grandma anymore?' he'd asked. Omar hated being collected from nursery by his grandmother, because that meant that he had to give up the comfort of riding in his mom's car and instead, had to catch the bus with his grandmother, as she didn't have a car and had never learnt to drive. He hated the long queue he had to join to get on the bus, and most of all, he hated having to stand in the cold to wait for its arrival.

'I'm sorry, Mommy,' replied Treasure, stretching out her hand to place it on her mommy's cheek. She felt that if it weren't for her and Omar, then her mother wouldn't have had to give up her job.

'There's no need for you to be sorry, baby,' said Cheryl as she placed her hand over that of her daughter's.

Sullivan drove anxiously to Cheryl's mother's house. He was eager to find out why Cheryl had been crying to put to rest his fears of how his brother had ended up in hospital. Cheryl was desperate to find out how Terry had attempted suicide, because she was convinced that's what he had done, but the two tried to put their own questions aside, since protecting the children from all the pain, uncertainty, and disruption that was around them was their priority, even as they tried to make sense of it all.

Cheryl returned to the waiting car within minutes of leaving her kids in her mom's care. She hadn't stopped to explain to her mother what had occurred, because she didn't wish to put her in a state of panic, especially since she couldn't be there to give her assistance with taking care of the two children.

'Why did the hospital ring you and not me?' questioned Cheryl, confused.

'The doctor who rang was a colleague of Terry's when he was a junior doctor, and he had my contact information since we've kept in touch over the years,' Sullivan tried to explain. Sullivan sensed that his sister-in-law wasn't comfortable with the idea of him being informed of her husband's hospitalisation before her, but that wasn't out of concern to him because he had more pressing issues on his mind. When Dr. Jessop had rung, he had said that Terry was unconscious and had suffered depression to his cranium. He wasn't sure of his prognosis, since at that point, they hadn't done the MRI. That had left Sullivan feeling as though someone had put a bullet through his heart.

Terry was the youngest of the three brothers, with Sullivan being a year older than him. The three brothers had always had a close bond, but Sullivan and Terry were particularly close, maybe because of the closeness in ages. They had no secrets, and even shared intimate details about their wives. He was scared to think that he wouldn't see his brother again, or that he wouldn't have the pleasure of his company out on the town anymore. The truth was, the thought of not having him around anymore really frightened him. There was so much he wanted to ask Cheryl—questions like, when was the last time you saw him? What was he doing at Bradgate Park at that time of night?

Why were you looking so distressed earlier? But the news of his brother's condition filled his thoughts.

Sullivan wasn't a religious man, but he found himself praying for his brother's speedy recovery. He was even tempted to ask Cheryl to ask her preacher dad to do an intercession to God on his behalf. Terry and his brothers had mocked Mr. Bradley on many occasions, especially when they were out drinking and they knew that he wouldn't approve of their behaviour, since he referred to any alcohol as the drink of the devil, and nightclubs and bars he called the devil's kingdom.

It was only this summer, after he and Terry had gone out to a club with a few of their friends to celebrate the birth of Terry's friend's new-born baby boy, that he and Terry began to mock Mr. Bradley after they'd had one too many bottles of cider. Terry had sprinkled some of his drink over Sullivan's head, pretending that it was holy water. 'I rebuke you, evil spirit, and I demand that you leave this young man's body free from your satanic drink!' he had said, imitating Mr. Bradley. But tonight he would have given anything just to have him lay his hands on his brother, and make him well again. He had witnessed him perform many miracles, and whilst he had been doubtful about his spiritual abilities in the past, tonight was the night that he was prepared to try the Lord through Reverend Bradley.

Cheryl sat quietly for most of the journey; she was angry with her husband for his betrayal of her, but ending up in a hospital bed was the last thing she would have wanted to happen to him. Just a few years ago, she was the envy of her friends, and her life seemed perfect, and she couldn't have asked for a more loving husband, a happier family, or a more fulfilling job. And now, catastrophe had struck, not just once, but several times. Her husband had started coming home late from work, whilst she suspected that he was having an affair, she never imagined that the woman she was sharing her husband with, was her own friend. She'd given up her job, at his request in an attempt to please him, and now he was in hospital, possibly fighting for his life.

During tragic moments like this, her grandmother would use the expression that 'this was God's wrath.' She'd normally defined God's wrath as a warning that one should turn from his wicked ways or face the continuous punishment. She wondered what sin she or Terry had committed to face such wrath, convinced that their plight was a warning from Him above.

'Lord, forgive us of our sins and help us to be better people as a couple and as individuals,' she prayed quietly.

They arrived at the hospital after visiting hours were over, but since word had gotten around the hospital that Terry was not only a doctor, but that he also had worked in that very hospital during his days as a trainee doctor, the red carpet was laid out for him. Sullivan and Cheryl were allowed onto the ward. Terry had been moved from the accident and emergency unit and was now on a ward for head injuries. The ward was quiet, with the exception of the sounds of beeping machines. Men and women could be seen with saline drips, blood pressure monitors, and oxygen masks attached to their bodies. Cheryl began to wonder what state Terry was in. Seeing a loved one with strings and machines hanging from his body can be very daunting, since it gives the impression that the patient is either very poorly off or at death's door.

Chapter 21

Going by the different uniforms, it was easy to determine the various roles each of the hospital staff played. The men and women dressed in blue overalls, which looked like sleepwear, were clearly doctors, since they walked around with their stethoscopes thrown around their necks. They seemed to do the least hands on-work, and were always accompanied by a man or woman dressed in navy blue trousers and a sky blue top. These were clearly the nurses, who could be overheard informing the doctors of this patient's progress and that one's setback. The nurses gave orders to women dressed in grey trousers and pink plaid tops. These were clearly the auxiliary staff, confirmed when a nurse shouted out to one of these women that the gentleman in bay five, bed number three, was incontinent of urine.

Before Cheryl and Sullivan reached the big desk situated in the middle of the ward, a petite black woman approached them and asked if she could be of assistance. She was polite enough, but she had a stern appearance, which most of the patients must have found intimidating, thought Cheryl. She had an African accent, not one that Cheryl recognised. Before either she or Sullivan could respond, a man rushed toward them.

'I'll see to them,' he stated. Cheryl turned in the direction of the voice and noted that it was one of the men who were wearing what looked like a pyjama.

'Thanks for ringing me,' said Sullivan. 'This is Terry's wife, Cheryl.'

Cheryl and the doctor exchange greetings. They followed the doctor to a room that was situated on the far side of the ward. It was comforting to see that Terry had been given his own room, but it was equally daunting, because single rooms were reserved for those with an infectious disease or those who were considered to be acutely unwell.

Cheryl gasped when she entered the room, seeing Terry hooked up to various machines, one which was his food supply, in the form of saline water. His eyes were closed, and he lay motionless.

'Is he asleep?' she asked, unaware that her husband was unconscious and had been since his accident. Doctor Jessop looked across at Sullivan and realised that he hadn't told Cheryl the full extent of her husband's injury. Neither man responded immediately, each waiting for the other to reply.

The doctor became uncomfortable with the silence and took Sullivan's lack of response as a way of telling him that he'd rather the doctor break the news to Cheryl.

'He's unconscious; he has been since the accident,' explained the doctor. Cheryl looked at her brother-in-law in alarm.

'He's in a coma?' she asked, with terror in her voice.

'He looks worse than he actually is,' replied the doctor calmly.

Cheryl looked at her brother-in-law for reassurance. Sullivan didn't speak—he couldn't—and he stood there in silence, with a blank look on his face.

He attended to many patients in this very hospital, and many lives depended on him in the past, and now here he is, he can't help save his own life, thought Sullivan.

Cheryl walked over to her husband's lifeless body. Just when she thought that she couldn't possibly cry anymore, because she had cried so much and figured she had run out of tears, tears streamed down her face as she reached out and rubbed his colourless cheek.

'I love you,' she murmured. 'Just come back to me, and I'll forgive everything that you've done.' She took his hand and placed it against her face, her tears dribbling down his hand, mirroring the drip in his tube.

His once-cold hand grew warm from her hot breath when she exhaled through her mouth.

'Terry! Oh Terry!' she stammered. 'There's nothing I wouldn't do to have you back! I love you—I always will!'

His index finger twitched against her face. She jumped in sheer astonishment, and she pulled his face from her hand to convince herself that this was so. But his fingers just lay still.

'Terry!' she screamed. 'Can you hear me?'

Sullivan hadn't seen his brother's finger move, but he knew by Cheryl's reaction that a marvel had just taken place.

From the doorway, where he'd been standing since they entered the room, he rushed over to his brother's bedside. He took hold of his brother's right hand and began to stare at it to see if he, too, could feel what Cheryl had felt.

'What just happened?' he asked quizzically.

'I felt his finger move,' she responded.

'Maybe you imagined it,' he said dubiously.

Cheryl threw herself at her husband in despair. She so desperately wanted him to open his eyes and take her in his arms. His infidelity had been forgotten, at least as far as she was concerned. A machine beeped as she lay across on his stomach, crying her heart out. She was startled by this and thought it meant his condition had deteriorated. She once again looked at Sullivan for reassurance. He could see the blood had drained from her face, for she feared the worse.

'It's just his drip; the nurse will come in to fix it,' he explained.

Before Cheryl could ask another question, a nurse popped into the room and restarted the drip. She explained to Cheryl that this was likely to happen about every fifteen minutes. Cheryl didn't seek clarification since she was relieved that the sound from the machine wasn't an indication that her husband had taken a sudden turn.

Sullivan left the room to find Jessop for some answers about his brother's prognosis, but there was something else that was bothering him. He wanted more details about the accident. Jessop told him all he knew, getting most of his information from the paramedics who had brought Terry into the hospital. This new information greatly confused Sullivan, because it didn't make sense for his brother to be out at that time of night or in the area where he had been found. He felt that Cheryl could shed some light on the situation, but she, too, was grieving for Terry. Although Sullivan was desperate to know what had transpired, he didn't wish to cause her any more woes. *I'll just let sleeping dogs lie*, he said to himself.

Chapter 22

Five hours later, Cheryl returned to her mother's house, where she had dropped the kids off with little explanation. She didn't know where to begin the story, because other than Trinny, no one knew about Terry's transgressions. How could she explain to her mother about his accident without telling her about what had led up to it? If the accident had occurred elsewhere, then maybe she would be able to just talk about it. But it had happened at Bradgate Park, where no one actually visited on his own, especially at that time of night. The park had a reputation for being a night-time meeting spot for lovers. *Mom will find this rather peculiar and would put two and two together and get a total of twenty-two*, she thought. She took a deep breath as she entered the door. She listened for a sign that the children were still awake, but it was as peaceful as a still river. *They must have gone to bed*, she said to herself.

She let herself in with the key she had from when she resided there. She was greeted by a row of toys. This sight would normally bring a smile to her face, but not today. A stab of pain rushed across her heart as she thought of how she'd explain to her children, that their daddy wasn't going to be coming home. The truth was, it frightened her because she didn't know if he would be coming home at all. She stepped in between the toys to avoid crushing them. She could hear water running from the tap in the kitchen, so she headed in that direction. Her mom's back was turned, so she hadn't seen her when she walked in.

Cheryl stood and stared at her mother. Her pain was so great, and whilst her mother had always offered a shoulder to cry on, she felt immense guilt about what she was about to off-load onto her. She knew that her mother would feel her pain as if it were her own.

Mrs. Bradley turned to look at her daughter. She was startled because she hadn't heard her when she came in, and she was dumbfounded by her appearance. Gone was the glamorous beauty who was always immaculately dressed. She had to be impeccable before she would leave the house. Her hair had to be worn a certain way; her makeup, this way; her clothing, that way; and here she was, looking worse for wear.

Mrs. Bradley gasped. 'Cheryl! Whatever is the matter?'

Cheryl tried her best to refrain from crying, but she just couldn't help it. She felt so physically weak, she was emotionally drained, and she really needed someone to help her through this horrible moment. Sullivan had seen her tears, but there was so much that she wanted to say but didn't feel she could share with him. Cheryl and Sullivan had a close relationship; he admired her as a woman, and she was respectable, hardworking, and committed to his brother. He always referred to her as a 'real lady.' She found him considerate and family-orientated, something that they both had in common, but she had never considered him as a confidant. That role was for her mother and sister, but she wished that she didn't have to share this particular burden with her mother. *It's going to kill you*, she said to herself.

Her knees gave way beneath her as her mother approached her to give her an embrace. Mrs. Bradley collapsed onto the floor beside her daughter, holding her daughter's face in her hands as she wept. 'My baby, my baby,' she cried, wiping away some of her daughter's tears with her thumb.

'Oh, Mom,' she spluttered.

Mrs. Bradley looked earnestly at her daughter, willing her on to share her pain and wishing that she could just take it all away from her. She didn't know what it was; all she knew was that her child was in anguish, great anguish, and she couldn't bear to see her like this. With tears rolling done her own face, she pulled her daughter's head forward so that it was buried in her bosom.

'God!' she cried out. 'Oh God, if it's your will, my God, if it's your will. Whatever has caused this pain to my child, I ask that you intervene right now and rectify the matter.'

Cheryl felt a sense of peace as these words were uttered. She didn't know whether this was because she knew the value of prayer or because she was desperate for a miracle, but she felt that her mother's prayer made a difference. She looked up at her mom like a helpless child. 'Thank you, Mom,' she said.

Mrs. Bradley looked at her daughter with pain-stricken eyes. 'I don't know what the problem is, and I won't force you to share it if you don't feel able to, but I've put you in the hands of God, and always will. He'll do the rest.'

Cheryl took her mother's hand and kissed it. It was this unconditional love and understanding that had given them such a strong bond. Her mother had never coerced her into doing anything that she didn't wish to do, not even during moments such as this one. But she had always given her support and left the door open for her to divulge her problems if and when she felt able to.

Cheryl explained to her mother about Terry's accident and what had occurred before the tragedy. Whilst her mother expressed her shock and sorrow on hearing that Terry had been in hospital, unconscious, she didn't seem surprised by what her daughter said about his unfaithfulness.

Cheryl furrowed her brows, curious. 'Mom, is there something that you know that you're not telling me?' she asked.

'I think you've had too much stress for one day,' replied the woman, attempting to digress. 'Let me get you something to eat. You must be hungry,' she further strayed.

'Mom,' Cheryl said in a stern voice.

'My child, some things are best left unsaid,' she exclaimed as she opened the fridge door to see what she could prepare for Cheryl.

But Cheryl insisted; she rose to her feet and followed her mother over to the fridge. 'Mom, please,' she begged. 'What is it that you're not telling me? Are you saying that you knew about them all along?'

Cheryl was perplexed by her mom's behaviour because she didn't know what to think. It would be impossible for her mother to keep such a secret from her, she thought.

Her mother looked at her with a disapproving look at the mention of this. 'Sit down,' she demanded. 'A few months after you got married, I had a vision, a vision about your marriage. Dare I say that it wasn't good?'

Mrs. Bradley went on to explain to Cheryl exactly what she had seen about her marriage. Her mother, like her grandmother, had been given a gift. They'd always believed that this gift was from God. They had the ability to see events and crisis whilst they were asleep, before they happened. Her mom had foreseen her getting married to a successful man a year prior to her meeting Terry, but she had never led her to believe that her marriage to him wouldn't be successful. Cheryl could understand why her mother had kept such a dream from her. Mrs. Bradley didn't always disclose her dreams about her kids, especially when she found them distressing, but she never forgot to say a prayer on their behalves, asking God to protect and deliver them, if it was His will.

Mrs. Bradley could see that her daughter was deep in thought. 'Cheryl,' she uttered.

Cheryl looked up at her mom, nervously. 'Do you think I made a mistake marrying him, Mom?'

'Every relationship has a rocky path,' she declared. 'It's how you handle it that determines your strength of character. I think he's a good man, but he's just lost his way.'

Cheryl was in agreement with her mom. She remembered how perfect she and everyone who knew Terry and the way he treated her, thought that he was. *You just can't pretend that*, she said to herself.

She barely touched the food that her mother had prepared for her. Her thoughts were with Terry and her kids. They were too old not to notice that their dad wouldn't be home, but too young to understand the concept of him being unconscious. She entered the room they were both sleeping in. Treasure was lying on her stomach, with one hand resting on her cheek; Omar was on his back, with his little legs taking up half the bed. She ran her fingers through his hair and kissed him on the forehead before turning to Treasure and stroking her fingers. 'Sleep tight, my little angels,' she muttered before leaving the room.

She arrived home to find a barrage of messages left on her cell phone. She skipped through them, with the exception of two; one was from Trinny, telling her that she was taking time off work so that she could be with her, and the other was from Sandy. Hearing her voice forced her to relive the scene of her and Terry all over again. But instead of feeling pain, Cheryl felt anger. Anger at the woman who had single-handedly destroyed her family, she thought. She blamed her for Terry's transgression; she blamed her for her tears that night; and, most of all, she blamed her for her husband's accident. To Cheryl, it was all Sandy's fault—Terry shared no part in it. Cheryl was about to pick up the receiver and ring the woman back to let her feel her wrath when the door bell rang.

She greeted her sister with an embrace that lingered for what seemed like an hour.

'He's unconscious, Trinny,' blurted out Cheryl as she pushed back from her sister's hug. 'I've seen him,' replied Trinny sympathetically.

'You went to see him?' queried Cheryl in astonishment.

Trinny worked on the maternity unit, just two floors below the admitting ward where Terry had been admitted. A nurse visiting from a neighbouring ward had told them that a doctor had been admitted into her ward on the night. Trinny had tuned in, curious at the mention of the word 'doctor,' especially after Cheryl had called her at 02.00 hours to inform her that Terry hadn't come home.

'What's the name of the doctor?' Trinny had asked.

'I believe his name is Odazzy,' replied the nurse.

'Odazic,' corrected Trinny.

'That's it,' replied the nurse.

Trinny had run off the ward as fast as she could, giving little explanation to her colleagues. She felt a lump come to her throat on seeing her brother-in-law lying motionless. She didn't like the man and hadn't for many years. His latest behaviour had added to her dislike for him, but she couldn't revel in his downfall, because the truth of the matter was that, his downfall was her beloved sister's downfall as well. And whilst he might have felt physical pain, it was her sister who was hurting emotionally, and the kids, who were too young to understand, would miss him terribly. Trinny had held her mouth and tried to fight back the tears, although one did escape and run down her face. *My dear Cheryl*, she thought to herself.

Trinny further explain to Cheryl how she was privy to knowledge about Terry's admission. Cheryl got washed and dressed, and the two women made their way back to the hospital. By now, news of Terry's admission had spread wide and far. His mother, father, and eldest brother Markus were by his side. Mrs. Odazic must have been crying, because her eyes were blood red and puffy. Mr. Odazic looked lost; he looked like a broken man. Cheryl had never seen him look this sad before. He was a proud man who had a reputation for being arrogant and boastful. He was condescending to people whom he thought weren't his equal. He came from a line of wealth. His forebears were entrepreneurs, and this wealth grew from generation to generation. He had never known what it was like to be poor or have to do without, and anyone who fell in that category he deemed worthless and lazy. His theory about wealth was that wealth didn't seek out anyone, but anyone who had the drive and determination to be wealthy could easily become so. Many people found his very presence intimidating. And there was Markus, who was the chatterbox out of the three brothers. It was impossible get a word in edgewise whenever he was around, since he liked to be the centre of attention. Tonight he didn't mind being overlooked.

Isn't it funny, how grief can change you, thought Cheryl.

Mrs. Odazic reached out and embraced Cheryl. 'How are you coping?' she asked cautiously.

'She's not,' retorted Trinny defiantly. Her sister was in turmoil in more ways than one, because of this woman's son, and she wasn't about to let her believe for a moment that it was easy for her. She knew that Cheryl would have lied and said that she was coping, because Cheryl always put others before herself. She would have walked in that room and become the counsellor, the friend, the listener, and even the tea lady if given the chance. Cheryl knew by her sister's reaction that she was livid, livid because the very man who had cause so much pain was, himself, unaffected by it all. He was too comatose to be aware of the devastation he had created. She was scared that Trinny might reveal all about the night he had the accident—not intentionally, because Trinny was ever loyal to her and wouldn't do anything against her wishes—in the heat of her anger, she might let something slip.

Cheryl turned to look at Trinny with a look of warning. 'I'm coping the best I can,' she said, staring at her sister.

Trinny could read her stare and knew she was giving her a warning. She was tempted to let the Odazic family know that their son-the-doctor wasn't a prince after all, but was a brute who had no respect for the sanctity of marriage or that of his wife, but her sister had suffered enough.

Mr. Odazic stared intensely at Trinny. He could sense that there was more to be told than Cheryl had let on. He could tell by his daughter-in-law's appearance that she had been quite distressed and had probably not eaten or had sufficient sleep; her eyes were red, she had dark, baggy circles under her eyes, and her protruding cheekbones were more pronounced than he'd ever known them to be. He wondered if, by Trinny saying that Cheryl wasn't coping, she'd meant that she was having a breakdown.

'Where are the kids?' he asked Cheryl with concern.

'They're well taken care of—they're with my mother,' replied Cheryl.

'How much of this do they know?' he asked, referring to Terry's physical state.

Cheryl paused, as if in a daze. She hadn't told the kids what had happened to their dad, and she didn't know how to.

She didn't want to paint him as a villain, but he was far from a saint, and although she had forgiven him for all that he had done, it hadn't taken the pain away.

'Cheryl?' asked Mr. Odazic, curious.

Cheryl jumped as if she had just been startled by an insect. 'Sorry. You were saying?'

The man looked at her with interest. He wasn't a doctor, and he had no medical background, but he'd taken a keen interest in Terry's work when he had had his placement on a psychiatric ward and would come home and share his experiences with him. He had asked many questions about the different forms of mental illnesses and their presentations, and now he had some understanding and second-hand knowledge of the nature of mental illness. But he sometimes over-read the symptoms in a bid to prove that he had acquired knowledge from his son. He had once given his wife a diagnosis of schizophrenia, because she had continuously told him that she could hear a noise in the attic that sounded like a cat. They didn't have a cat and, for the forty years that they had lived in the house, had never had a cat, not even a stray or one accompanying visitors. But his wife was convinced that there was a cat in the house, only she'd never seen it, and he'd never heard the crying sounds that she so often complained about.

He had called Marcus to tell him about his concern for his mother. Marcus was angry at his dad for even harbouring such a thought.

'Schizophrenia!' he'd bellowed at his dad. As soon as he'd put the phone down, he'd made a call to Terry. That night, the three boys went to see their parents. Their mom being labelled a schizophrenic wasn't something that they were about to take lightly, not only because they knew too well the stigma that went with such a label, but also because they knew that there would be a strong chance that one of the three of them would have the disorder too.

They rebuked their dad and were appalled that a man would be so quick to give his wife such a label, especially when they discovered that the neighbour's cat had actually let itself into the attic and must have been there for days, since the attic was filled with its excrement and a strong smell of its urine. Mrs. Odazic was oblivious to her husband's perception of her mental state, and the boys never told her because they knew that she'd be vey hurt by her husband's comment.

Mrs. Odazic had developed postnatal depression after Terry was born, and whilst she had wanted to have six children, she had decided to not have any more after Terry's birth. She was frightened at what she had become during the time she suffered from postnatal depression. Although she recovered quickly and returned to her normal self, she was worried that having more children would cause her to have the disorder again; her physician had told her that her chances of developing the illness again after childbirth were increased.

Mr. Odazic found Cheryl anxious and distracted, but now wasn't the time to enquire about her mental health, he thought. *She needs our support now, more than ever*, he muttered to himself. He didn't wish to ask any more questions about the kids out of fear that Cheryl might see through him, so he digressed.

'Mary and I can take the kids off your hands, to give you and your mom a bit of rest,' he expressed.

'That's kind of you, but we're okay for now,' she replied.

Chapter 23

Terry lay motionless, with the noise from the machine that was supplying his fluid intake making the only sound in the room. It was hard for his family to grasp and accept his position. He hadn't been sick or even complained about a headache; he was a healthy man who, just days ago, was trying to save lives. Now, here he was.

Cheryl took a kidney bowl from one of the shelves just above his head and filled it with water before taking some of the cotton wool, which was left in the room earlier by his attending nurse, and wiped his lips. They had become dry from him not taking in any food or fluid orally.

She ran her finger across his lips. This brought her back to their honeymoon. She had laid on top of him, caressing, feeling, and exploring his body, whilst he lay beneath her, with the beat of his heart making the only sound or movement from him. He was so captivated by her that he had become speechless—but he hadn't needed any speech, since the expression in his eyes said it all.

With tears flowing down her face, she threw her body onto his, her face directly above his, her nose facing his nose, her lips against his, and she sobbed. Trinny went to pull her back, not out of concern for Terry, but because she could see how distraught her sister was by seeing her husband in such a lifeless position. She wanted to take her away from it all, but she was intercepted by Terry's mom. She felt that it was important that Cheryl be given the chance to grieve for her husband, and that he be able to hear her, since this might aid in his recovery. Although Terry was unable to speak or move, Mrs. Odazic felt that he knew they were present and could hear every word they said. And she was correct in her thoughts. As Cheryl tears began to dribble onto Terry's lips, his mouth spontaneously opened, and his tongue protruded briefly, as to taste her tears. Cheryl was oblivious to this because she was so beside herself with grief. Mrs. Odazic gasped and leapt forward, grabbing her eldest son's hand to lead him toward his brother. Mr. Odazic followed his wife and son and placed his hand on her shoulder in awe.

'Look, Mary! Look!' he said in disbelief. Trinny reached forward and placed her arm around her sister, who was now facing her. Cheryl could tell by everyone's reaction that something had happened, but she wasn't sure what.

'He just opened his mouth,' exuded Trinny.

'And licked your tears,' added Marcus.

Cheryl swiftly turned to look at her husband, but once again, he was in his comatose position.

She took his face in her hands, and in despair, she pleaded. 'Darling if you can hear me, I just want you to know how much I love you. We all do, and we're all here praying for you.'

His eyes flickered.

'Terry!' she squealed.

He opened his eyes. The nurses and doctors on the ward all rushed in to investigate the source of jubilation that was coming from Terry's room. They never doubted that he would recover; his prognosis was good. He'd also received the best medical and nursing care that a patient could ever have wished for, but they hadn't anticipated such a quick recovery. They looked on in amazement.

Terry looked around the room in a trance; he didn't seem to recognise anyone in the room. Jessop, the doctor who had informed Sullivan of his admittance, was one of the doctors who rushed to the room. He stepped forward to examine his friend.

'Could you all leave the room!' he demanded, and with the exception of Nurse Denise, everyone departed.

Cheryl looked up in amazement. 'Even me?' she asked.

'Even you, Cheryl,' he declared.

They were escorted to a family waiting room, which was halfway down the ward. Whilst there, Mr. Odazic began to wonder if his earlier perception about his daughter-in-law was wrong. He began to see her in a totally different light—she was no longer a distracted, anxious woman, but a woman who had a deep and sincere love for his son, a love that was so strong it brought him out of his unconsciousness.

Cheryl and the other two women held each other's hand while they awaited news from the doctor. Marcus paced the floor, back and forth, because he couldn't stop himself from pacing. One minute he had been wondering if his brother would ever make it alive out of this hospital, and then, within minutes, Terry's eyes were open and they had been told to leave the room, without any explanation given.

'What's taking them so long?' he said indignantly.

Jessop entered the room. They all looked at him in great anticipation.

'I have some good news,' he explained. 'Terry has aroused from his state of unconsciousness.'

The three women embraced each other, Mr. Odazic stood to his feet, and Marcus stopped pacing and listened attentively. He sensed a 'but' coming on.

The doctor continued, 'But I'm afraid you won't all be able to see him because he's not ready yet for so many visitors. He is, however, asking to see his wife.'

All heads turned to look at Cheryl. No one could disagree with this. She was his wife and the mother of his children, so it was only fitting that he would request to see her. She was also responsible for awakening him from his coma.

Cheryl entered the room to meet her husband's stare. He smiled wryly at her. She rushed over and threw herself at him.

'Take it easy, he's still a sick man' said the doctor jokingly.

'Don't you ever scare me like that again,' commanded Cheryl. She filled him in on how he had been for the past two days and how she'd cried until she had no more tears left to shed.

'I heard most of it,' explained Terry, referring to the conversation his wife had with him, during his state of unconsciousness, and the level of commitment and love she had shown throughout. Because whilst he was unable to respond, he said, 'It was you who gave me the strength to pull through.'

Cheryl was taken aback by this. 'You were unconscious,' she said, astonished.

'I wasn't brain-dead, Cheryl. My brain just wouldn't allow me to do certain functions, but it never took away my ability to hear,' he said with a smile. She took his hand and placed it on her cheek.

'That's my cue to leave,' said Dr. Jessop. 'I'll pop in on you later.'

'I'm so sorry,' he said, making an apology for his infidelity. She put one finger to his mouth to silence him.

'Not now,' she demanded.

He was only too glad to not have to explain to her about the night in question. He knew that, eventually, the time to do so would come eventually, but for now, he just wanted to relish the peaceful moment he had with his wife. He sensed that a storm was brewing, but he didn't want to face it whilst he was so weak. Cheryl was like a defending barrister in court when she wanted answers to her questions. She could be fierce and persistent, too, when she thought that the perpetrator wasn't being totally honest, and he knew that he had to be sharp, strong, and be prepared for her interrogation. He had told her on many occasions that she was in the wrong job, that she could easily have become a solicitor.

Terry didn't have much memory of his accident, so there was a gap between him leaving home that night and ending up in Bradgate Park. Cheryl was curious as to what had transpired;

she wasn't sure whether he had attempted to end his own life or whether it was an accident, but she wasn't going to feed her curiosity. Her husband had made it past death's door, and she was just pleased to have him back.

Terry was discharged two days later. Whilst he was nervous and unsure about their future as a family, Cheryl carried on as if nothing had happened. She played the role of a caring and loving wife, unconditionally. The kids later learnt that their daddy was a bit sick and had to spend some time with the doctor. Treasure seemed to understand this very well, and she'd oftentimes look at her daddy's burned back and ask him when the doctors would be able to make it better. But Omar was totally confused—he couldn't understand how a doctor could become sick, since they were the ones who helped the sick to get well; he couldn't understand why his dad would need to see a doctor when he was a doctor himself.

Six weeks went by, and Terry's wounds healed nicely. He hadn't encountered any further symptoms from his head injury.

'You're looking well, doc,' expressed the doctor who examined Terry on one of his out-patient appointments. 'A few more weeks, and you'll be ready to return to work. Perhaps you could take my place and let me have a rest,' he said, teasing.

Terry gave a hearty laugh and turned to look at his wife for a reaction, but she had a solemn face. He was taken aback by her expression because he'd expected her, more than anyone else, to be pleased that he was in good health—or almost in good health.

They left the clinic in utter silence, with Cheryl refusing to make eye contact with her husband. He stared at her for most of the journey back to the car to see if she would give anything away, for the one thing that Cheryl was poor at was being discreet about how she was feeling. Her face was a mirror of her emotions, and Terry could always tell what she was thinking or how she was feeling just by looking at her. When they arrived at the car, he tentatively opened the door for her. He now felt that he was in danger and was treading on thin ice.

'Do you want to tell me what the matter is?' he asked his wife cautiously.

Cheryl didn't respond immediately. She turned her head away from him and stared through the window. He was anxious to know what to do because he didn't want to drive the car whilst she was in that mood, nor did he want to push her too much for an answer, afraid it might escalate into a public row. He sat for a while with his head bowed, just playing with his car keys. Cheryl still didn't respond. He sensed by her behaviour that whatever it was, it was something great, and his mind flashed back to the night in question.

They arrived home without exchanging a word with each other. He felt more comfortable and confident since no amount of shouting would create a scene for others to stare at; now it was just the two of them, in the privacy of their own home.

'Cheryl!' he said more forcefully. 'What's the matter? I thought you'd be pleased about my recovery, and even more pleased that I'm well enough to be able to return to work.'

She looked at him with pain in her eyes. Her pain was so poignant that he was able to see and feel it.

'I'm elated by your recovery,' she said. 'But I can't pretend that I'm happy about you going back to work.'

'Cheryl, I …' She put her hand up and stopped him before he could finish his sentence.

'Whilst you're here,' she continued, 'I know that you're not with that tart,' she said angrily.

Terry looked away from her. He knew the day would come when they would have to talk about that night, but he found it extremely embarrassing to talk about it to the very woman who had caught them. If she had heard about his transgression, then it would be far easier to discuss, but she had caught him with her own eyes. She knew every position that they had taken that night … she was aware of all the details.

How does a man begin to explain to his wife about him and his private parts being found in another woman's mouth?' he said to himself.

He sat down opposite her, with his hands clasped together as if in a pleading position, and he leant forward in his chair, his voice breaking with emotion when he spoke. 'I'm begging for your forgiveness,' he said, imploringly.

With tears streaming down her face, she spluttered, 'If I hadn't forgiven you, do you think I would have nursed you through your illness? I've forgiven, but my God, it hurts. I want to know how long you've been seeing her, where, and when.' She stopped as if she'd just seen a ghost. 'Do you love her?' she asked fearfully.

'Oh God, no! No!' he said emphatically.

Terry began to tell his wife about the start of his affair. He was candid and honest because he knew Cheryl's interrogation would only prove him to be a liar, if he should do so. She would catch him out if he were less than truthful. He reached out for her hands when he saw that the information was too painful for her to hear, but she pulled her hands back defiantly.

'What's wrong with me?' she asked.

He fumbled with this question, for unless he wanted to be a dead man, there was no way he could tell his wife the truth about why he'd often gone to Sandy for blow jobs.

She stared at him impatiently; he bowed his head in disgrace. 'I didn't think you liked doing that,' he said in a mere whisper.

She was aghast to discover that there were women in this world who were prepared to perform such acts on men who weren't their husbands. She was even more aghast to learn that some women would do just that, without the pleasure being returned. She asked if his affair with Sandy was one of the reasons he demanded that she leave her job.

'That had nothing to do with my wanting you home,' he declared.

Cheryl's interrogation carried on for the next four hours, and if she hadn't had the kids to collect from school and nursery, it could well have carried on into the night. She expressed to her husband that whilst she loved him, she'd lost a fundamental ingredient in their marriage, and that was trust.

Terry returned to work two weeks later, under the watchful eyes of his wife. Cheryl would ring him on the hour at work, and if he missed her call, he was expected to return it; if he didn't, he ended up spending the night with the devil on his return home.

Cheryl's health deteriorated when Terry returned to work; she was notably anxious and forgetful. She wasn't sleeping at nights, and Terry would often wake during the night to find her and their bed clothing wet with perspiration. The first night it occurred, he was baffled as to why his wife had perspired so much in the middle of winter. Even more confusing was the fact that Cheryl never broke out in a glow of sweat, even in the sweltering heat.

He turned over one night to wrap his arms around her, as he had done on many nights, to find that he was grasping a wet body, and when he opened his eyes to awaken her, he found that the wetness had extended to the bedclothes underneath both of them. His first thought was that his wife had had an accident during the night and was too deep in sleep to notice.

'Cheryl, Cheryl,' he whispered as he shook her from her sleep.

As she roused from her sleep, she realised that the only patch of dry clothing on her was the crotch of her knickers. They had both dismissed this as a one-off incident wherein Cheryl's body had become overheated because of the heating system in the house. Cheryl, of course, knew that this wasn't the case, since she had been experiencing tremors in her hands and legs for the past four days. Going down the stairs one morning, she had felt her legs become weak, and then they started shaking. She had experienced this later that same day, while she was preparing breakfast for the kids, and she had had to reach for the table for support out of fear of falling. She had seen her hands tremble on many occasions through the day, especially when they were unsupported, and she knew that this could be the result of one of two things. She knew it had to be either a physical problem, such as her thyroid, or it had to be a mental problem, such as anxiety. And she was convinced that it was the latter. Her memory was a problem too; although she was able to remember events that had taken place years ago, she struggled to recall those that occurred just minutes ago.

Terry suggested that she get some psychiatric input, which wasn't well received. He recommended that she be seen by a private doctor, as opposed to her general physician, since this wasn't something that they wanted on her medical records out of fear that the stigma that could follow her, as well as affect other aspects of her life, such as restarting employment.

'I'll pay for you to go private,' he exclaimed.

'There's nothing wrong with me,' she fired back.

'You're not right!' he said indignantly.

'You just want me carted off so you can carry on with your floozies,' she responded angrily.

Her symptoms became increasingly worse. Terry wasn't able to answer her calls on busy days at work, and he wasn't able to return them either. One day, an explosion had gone off in London, and doctors from neighbouring counties were doing their very best to help the injured. People were lying in the streets, with blood pouring from them. The emergency service was overstretched, and Terry was one of many doctors who had been airlifted to London to help with this disaster. London had never experienced anything of its nature. It brought back the dreadful memories of September 11. The country had been brought to its knees. Everyone and anyone who had a heart beating inside them, even if it was a pacemaker, stopped to give whatever help they could, and the dear Lord knew that it was needed.

On his arrival home that day, Terry found Cheryl at the window, looking out for him, but it wasn't this behaviour that startled him. She was wet and clammy as if someone had poured ice water over her, and she was hyperventilating too. She grabbed hold of his arm and attempted to speak, but the words weren't able to flow through.

Terry looked at her in astonishment. He knew that his wife had a problem, but he hadn't acknowledged the severity. He took hold of her in a bid to explain his whereabouts, but this was to no avail, because Cheryl's rate of hyperventilation increased. He switched on the television, knowing the incident in London was making headline news.

'Look!' he said in frustration. 'That's what I've been seeing to all day.'

Cheryl's eyes were now fixed on the television screen, but the rate of her breathing was still rapid. He took his wife's hand and led her to the sofa. With his eyes fixed on hers, he made attempts to relax her.

'Deep, slow breaths, Cheryl. Deep, slow breaths,' he advised.

Cheryl's breathing was less erratic, and she looked at the television in disbelief. 'When did this take place?' she asked.

'Midday today,' replied Terry.

'I had no idea,' she answered. 'Was it the work of a terrorist?' she asked.

'We aren't sure at this time.' He looked at his wife with concern while she focused on the news. He acknowledged that she needed help; the type of help that even he, as a doctor and her husband, wouldn't be able to provide. He was racked with guilt because if it hadn't been for his infidelity, his wife's mental health would have remained intact.

'Cheryl,' he called attentively, 'I want you to see a psychiatrist.'

She looked at him, perplexed.

He was expecting her to erupt in anger, since this had always been her response, but to his surprise, she reacted like a fearful child. With both his hands enclosed in hers, she pleaded. 'Don't do this, Terry. Please, don't send me away.'

'You're not going anywhere, Cheryl, but you do need to see someone,' he explained.

Like a petulant child, she stuck out her bottom lip and looked at him defiantly. 'I won't, Terry,' she declared.

Terry had become frustrated by now, as he had seen his wife's mental health rapidly deteriorated since his discharge from hospital. He knew with her continuous worry and fear, she was likely to sink even further, and there was nothing he himself could do at home to treat her. Her illness wasn't his speciality. But he was fearful for her; he worried that she would lose the respect that she'd gained from those around her. People were far less empathetic toward someone with a mental illness than they were toward someone with cancer or a broken bone. The general public opinion about people with mental disorders was that they should be locked away in some form of asylum. They were considered as a threat to society, too dangerous to have as a neighbour. But there was something else that greatly bothered Terry—he blamed himself for Cheryl's predicament.

'I will force you, if I have to, Cheryl, but please, don't make me take that route,' he begged.

She was aghast at his statement because she knew only too well what he was implying.

'You wouldn't dare!' she roared. 'If you had kept your dick in your pants and not in some tart's mouth, I would never …' She stopped herself from finishing her statement. She came so close to admitting that she had a mental illness, something that she had never done before, and it frightened her.

'I'll do what I have to do to protect you,' replied Terry calmly. 'And if that means getting you admitted under a section, then so it is.'

With tears filling her eyes, all she could do was stare at him. Not only was he her next of kin, who could make a recommendation for a mental health assessment on her behalf according to the mental health act, but he was also a doctor. A well-respected profession, that status alone was enough to get two doctors and an approved social worker to assess her mental health, she thought to herself. She could tell by the look in his eyes that he was serious.

'What do you want me to do?' she asked.

'I'm taking you to see my friend, who's a psychiatrist at a private hospital in London. He's known to be one of the very best in his field,' he declared.

Chapter 24

It had been two days since Terry spoke to Des, his psychiatrist friend. He hadn't gone into details about Cheryl's condition over the phone, but he'd expressed to his friend that he was concerned enough about her to ask for his help.

Des was a short, medium-built man whose skin was as dark as his hair. He was astoundingly handsome, and when he smiled, he lit up the room, for his teeth were as white as dairy milk. They were so perfect and bright that it would be hard not to think that he'd had some form of cosmetic work done.

Terry had arranged to meet him outside of work, and Des had agreed to meet them in a room at the Claridges' Hotel so as not to arouse any suspicion. Des was casually attired; gone were his usual jacket and tie, replaced by denim jeans and a navy blue T-shirt.

Terry returned to the room with Des after being informed by the receptionist that there was a visitor waiting for him in the lobby. Cheryl was unnerved by Des. She'd had many encounters with psychiatrists and doctors, both through her line of work and through Terry. But never in her wildest dreams did she ever think she'd reach a stage in her life when she would need her mental health assessed by one.

Before they had Treasure, Terry would have regular nights out with his colleagues from work. They had organised barbeques, taking turns to host one at their homes. It was through these, that she had discovered how pompous and self-indulgent doctors could really be. One doctor ranted about how his patients were there to take instructions from him. If they dared to challenge his diagnosis or his treatment plan, he asked them to leave his clinic and treat themselves, accusing them of thinking that their knowledge was superior to his. Another bragged about how he'd struck a patient off his register because she asked to seek a second opinion. Of course, he hadn't let it be known to his colleagues that this was the case; instead, he'd told them that he found the woman to be very abusive toward him and therefore found it difficult to continue to have her as his patient, because he felt threatened by her.

Cheryl stood up from her seated position to greet Des. He smiled at her, displaying his dazzling white teeth. She greeted him with a hug that was insincere, it made Des felt uncomfortable. It wasn't standard protocol to meet potential patients in a hotel room and give them his opinion about their mental health, but he'd agreed to do so because he'd been a friend of Terry's father and had known Terry since he was born. He had played pool with Terry's father, eaten dinner at their table, and had slept in their house on many occasions. He had even had the privilege of being seated in the front row at their wedding, an honour that is normally bestowed, upon relatives. Terry had come to love Des.

Now, here Des was, perhaps about to break the worst news to Terry about the woman he loved. He could tell by Cheryl's body language and the manner with which she greeted him, that she resented his help and perhaps saw him as being an interfering man, who had nothing better to do than to seek out the unstable.

Des started informally chitchatting, trying to break the ice. He asked about the kids and her new role as a housewife. She flinched at this question.

I see where the root of the problem is, said Des to himself.

Terry was getting frustrated at his question; he was desperate for Des to assess Cheryl's mental state and give them a diagnosis and a treatment plan. In his line of work, that was how it was done: an examination to find the source of the problem, followed by a diagnosis and possible prognosis, and then a treatment plan. He failed to comprehend that the minute Des walked in the room, his assessment had begun, and every question he'd asked Cheryl had given him an insight into the state of her mental health.

After what seemed like an interrogation to Cheryl and a waste of time to Terry, Des turned to Terry. 'So what's your concern?' he asked the younger man.

Terry gave Des the details that he thought were necessary. He hadn't told his friend how his wife would call him on the hour at work, and would work herself into a state if he didn't respond immediately, because he was sure the older man would ask him to divulge what had caused her to be so distrustful of him. Terry was a man who loved to be liked and respected by those around him. He couldn't bear to lose that respect, and if he let it slip to Des about his extramarital affairs, he'd knew that before long, he'd have his father on the other end of the phone berating him. He could see the disappointment in his mother's eyes and the embarrassment felt by his brothers.

He also hadn't told Des that his wife was now experiencing visual and auditory hallucinations, because that would be admitting that she was really mad, and he didn't wish to bestow this label on his wife, his kids, and himself. Anxiety and depression were considered common mental health problems; they were so common that one in four individuals was said to experience one or the other at some point in his or her life. And whilst he suspected that his wife was suffering from one of these, he had to accept that there was a possibility that she had more than just a common mental disorder, because she had psychotic symptoms too.

His memory went back to his days as a junior doctor on the psychiatric wards, when he saw many professionals, including doctors and lawyers, admitted. Every one of them was petrified of the ramifications, if his disorder were to become public knowledge. 'It would destroy my family, my profession. I'm as good as dead,' one man had said to him. So although Terry wanted his wife to receive treatment, he didn't want it to backlash on her or his family, so he was selective about the details he gave about her symptoms, making every effort not to sound critical or disrespectful. He spoke as a caring, loving husband who was acting out of concern for his wife.

Cheryl sat and looked at the two men as they discussed her, talking as if she weren't in the room. For her, it was like sitting in a ward round, when the doctors and nurses and other professionals would congregate and discuss their patients. This time, though, she was the patient. Measures had been taken to rearrange the format of ward rounds on the ward after several patients had complained that they found the format intimidating. Present would be a consultant and his junior doctor, a nurse from the ward, a nurse from the community, a social worker, a pharmacist, and two or three student doctors. The patients had requested that they be seen only with their consultant and a ward nurse. She had described this as being absurd. 'Every member of the team has a vital role. Without the input of the varied professionals, patients' care would be jeopardised,' she had declared. Now she could empathise with them.

Here she was, in the presence of her own husband and a man who was considered to be 'family,' and she found the experience to be daunting and demeaning.

'I think with a bit of sleep and some form of family therapy, Cheryl should be as right as rain,' expressed the older man. He didn't say that he suspected that there were some marital problems, and whilst her lack of employment was one component of the problem, he sensed that there were other issues too. 'It's not easy for a career-minded individual, to suddenly adapt and adjust to the role of being a house-husband or a housewife,' he further explained. 'I sense that Cheryl needs to have some form of activity outside of the home that will be meaningful to her. I'll write you a prescription for some zopiclone and lorazepam. The zopiclone …'

He stopped midway in his sentence, when he saw that Cheryl gave him a look. It was a look that he could read and understand only too well. She was a pharmacist by profession; she had far more knowledge and understanding of medications than he did. There was no need for him to go into a teaching session.

Cheryl's face lit up at his reaction; it was good to see that someone still respected her ability as a pharmacist. By Des leaving her to make the decision about the medication that he prescribed, he was saying to her that she still had credibility, even as a retired pharmacist, and he trusted her enough to use her knowledge. This meant the world to Cheryl. She embraced the man, this time with a warmer hug. He'd respected and believed in her over the years, and it was comforting to see that even though she had lost some aspect of her former self, she hadn't lost his respect and his belief in her.

'You must get plenty of rest,' said the older doctor before he left the room.

Terry took his wife into his arms and held her as tight as it was possible to do without causing her any harm. Zopiclone and lorazepam were confirmation to him that his wife had a problem, a problem that was not likely to rectify itself on its own.

'So what do you think of family therapy?' asked Terry after he released her.

'We don't need therapy,' she declared. 'We shouldn't have to feel the need to sit in front of a complete stranger and disclose our deepest secrets in order to understand each other. We can do that by ourselves.'

Chapter 25

They arrived in the Caribbean, to the very place where it had all begun. This was the place where they had started their married lives; it held so many profound and romantic memories. Cheryl spent two weeks not needing lorazepam or zopiclone; she was hundreds of miles away from her problems. Sandy was back in England, and her husband was by her side every minute of the day; she always knew where he was and what he was doing. Terry could see the difference in his wife. There were no stressors in the Caribbean to raise her anxiety level, and there was no repeat of her hallucinations, which had been caused by her lack of sleep and exhaustion. He was relieved to see that her disorder was reactive, not generic, because by being reactive, eradicating the stressors, sorted out the problem.

Terry suggested that they move to the Caribbean, but although this was doable, it was unrealistic. It would mean uprooting the kids and taking them from everything they knew and loved. They'd be hundreds of miles away from their grandparents, aunties and uncles, and the friends that they had formed both in nursery and school.

'This would affect the kids too much,' emphasised Cheryl. She'd ruled out the possibility of returning to work as well, being apprehensive about Terry's ability to cope with her being independent. Her thoughts went back to the days when her marriage was at its worst. She recalled the abuse she suffered at the hands of her own husband, his disappearing acts, and the impact they'd had have on the children, and a chilling feeling shot through her stomach. *I can't face that again,* she said to herself.

She felt a tinge of embarrassment when she recalled the night that helped destroy her mental health, and knew she could never return to her former place of employment … not to rub shoulders with Sandy.

Terry agreed that he'd find work closer to home, since knowing he was close by might give her some security. He also agreed to leave her to form and maintain her relationships with her friends, and to accept the close relationships that she had with her sister and her mother. Cheryl was dubious about his promises; after all, he'd made them before, only to break them. *But at least it's a start,* she said to herself.

They flew back to England, intending to start over; ahead lay a hard task. Terry knew that returning to England, where the centre of the problem was, would be a test for his wife. He was apprehensive about how much of an impact his changing jobs would have on Cheryl's mental health. The major problem was his infidelity, and the only way he could convince her that he was committed to their marriage wasn't by his apology or shortening the distance between his job and his home, but by his behaviour over time, and this would take time. He had a lot to prove, but what would happen to Cheryl's already-fragile state in the meantime? And there was Sandy, the woman lived in the same county as they did; they were bound to meet her at some point. How would Cheryl cope with this? He wished he could erase the day Cheryl had found him with Sandy, for whilst she had suspected that he was cheating from his late nights returning home. It was the incident that had occurred at Cheryl's leaving do that had triggered this episode of mental illness. The blame was at his front door, and was far easier for him to create this upheaval, but was proving rather difficult to rectify it. *What a mess*, he thought.

Trinny stopped in to see her sister on her return from the Caribbean. She was the only one, other than Terry and her mother, who knew about her sister's problems, and she hated him for it. She held him responsible, and she was so angry for the distress that he had caused her sister, that she was tempted to hire a hit man to kill him. But the thought of robbing her niece and nephew of their dad stopped her. She tried to convince Cheryl to leave Terry. But Cheryl, who had tried leaving him before—and had to return— realized that the life she so desired for her and her kids wasn't achievable without him.

'It's better to live a life of a squalor and have good health than to live like a Saudi princess and be nuts,' said Trinny angrily.

Terry started a new, local job. He popped home in between seeing his patients at the clinic, in part to check on Cheryl, and partly because he wanted to deter her from getting herself in a state by thinking he was having an affair. This seemed to be effective, since in the eight weeks since they'd returned from the Caribbean, other than Cheryl having to occasionally take a few zopiclone to help her sleep, she hadn't experienced any more anxiety-related symptoms.

She had met up with Angel in Birmingham on a few occasions, and had done what they called 'therapeutic shopping.' She had spent over two thousand pounds, buying clothes for herself and her children, and every pound was charged to her husband's credit card. The two women had joked about how rewarding it was to be a housewife.

'I'd trade my place for your's any day,' said Angel joyfully. 'I work five days a week, nine hours per day, and I don't get two thousand pounds at the end of the month. Here you are, a housewife, spending two thousand pounds of your husband's money.'

Cheryl had returned home that day in the best of moods. Meeting up with Angel was always one of her favourite social events. Angel was witty and funny, and she knew how to have fun.

Cheryl spent more and more time visiting her friends and family. Terry was happy for her because he could see how beneficial having a social circle was to her mental health. She had returned to the Cheryl he met and fell in love with. But he was getting worried. He sensed that Trinny wasn't happy with their reunion, having inside information about his treatment of Cheryl in the past, more than he'd like for her to have. He feared that she'd used the close relationship that she has with Cheryl to tear them apart. He knew the two most influential people in Cheryl's life were Trinny and their mother. *Combined, they could pull my family apart*, he thought to himself.

He returned home from work one afternoon to find an empty house. He rang Cheryl's mobile to find out where she was.

'Hi darling!' he said when Cheryl answered. 'Where are you?'

'Oh, I'm at Trinny's,' she replied.

'I'm home,' he said.

'Okay, I'll see you later.

Terry was aghast at her response; he had expected her to immediately gather the kids and return home, as she would normally do, but instead, she stayed at her sister's for another three hours before returning home. He saw this as being Trinny's influence. He so much wanted to destroy the bond between the two women, but he knew he would have to have a well-planned strategy to do so, or he'd risk losing his wife.

He hid his disappointment when Cheryl walked through the door. He embraced her tenderly before turning to play with his kids.

'Did you have lots of fun at Aunty Trinny's?' he asked playfully.

That night, Terry proved to be a super husband and dad. He ran Cheryl a bath, and helped to bath and settled their two kids for the night, before sitting down with his wife and pampering her.

He had increased the number of his visits home from work in an attempt to prevent Cheryl from visiting Trinny or from Trinny visiting her. Trinny would never visit the house when he was around, and if he happened to return home when she was visiting, she'd terminate her visit. He found her behaviour to be disrespectful and rude toward him, but he dared not complain, because Cheryl would defend her sister's honour.

Terry and Trinny used to be the best of friends; she was the sister that he never had. Their relationship started to deteriorate, however, after Cheryl resigned from work, and it had further broken down after that 'cursed night.' Now it seemed it was beyond repair.

'Don't you think that Donavan mind you spending so much time at his house?' he asked Cheryl after she returned from Trinny's one evening.

'Why would he?' asked Cheryl with a frown on her face.

'You seem to spend all your time there. When does he get time to spend with his wife?' he said firmly.

Cheryl stopped to digest the remarks. She loved spending time with her sister, and her sister, likewise, enjoyed having her around. Treasure and Omar relished the time they spent with their cousins because they didn't have many friends outside of nursery and school. To be able to play with their cousins each afternoon after school was like heaven to them. But she'd never thought about the impact this had on her sister's husband. He was away most of the time for work, so he hardly saw his family; and when he did have the chance to be with them, there was never any privacy. She realised that more often than not, he had to share her with her and her kids.

She was brought out of her reverie by Terry's voice. 'Does he still work away, on the lorries?' he asked.

'He comes home every fortnight,' replied Cheryl.

'There's not a lot of quality time there,' expressed Terry in an attempt to get his point across to his wife more clearly.

'I suppose,' she replied with a tinge of guilt.

Trinny was puzzled as to why her sister's visits were becoming less and less frequent, and Cheryl no longer seemed to welcome having her around.

'The kids miss not having Treasure and Omar to play with as often as they used to,' stated Trinny, searching her sister's face for clues to answer to her question.

'I just feel like I'm taking up all your time,' Cheryl expressed. 'Donavan works away most days, and when he returns, I'm sure he'd like to be able to spend his time with you and your kids. I'm like an imposter.'

'Did Donavan tell you this?' asked Trinny, curiously. 'He wouldn't, would he? And I suppose you want to spend your time with Terry, so that's the reason behind you being so unwelcoming,' she said indignantly.

Cheryl gazed at her sister, furiously, because she knew that her remarks were directed at her husband, as she could sense that her sister was indirectly implying that Terry had return to his controlling behaviour.

'What's that look for?' retorted Trinny.

Cheryl turned to face her sister. 'He's not all bad you know,' she said firmly.

'What part of him isn't?' retorted Trinny, furiously. 'He forced you to give up a decent job, cut you off from your friends, cheated on you with your own friend, and caused you to develop a mental disorder, and you stand there and defend him.'

Cheryl was appalled at her sister's brutal honesty, and now wished she hadn't divulged so much to her because, in doing so, she had caused her husband and her sister to become enemies, and this wasn't a comfortable position for her to be in, because she loved them both.

Chapter 26

Cheryl stopped to look at the woman who was standing by the cash machine. Her back was turned to Cheryl so she was unable to satisfy her curiosity. The woman's hair was an auburn red colour, different from the dark brown it was before. From behind, she looked as though she had gained at least three stone in weight. Terry followed his wife's eyes and found Sandy. He recognised her immediately, since he'd seen her just before they went on holiday. The woman had turned up at his place of work to enquire why he hadn't been taking or returning her calls. He had been shocked to see how much she'd changed in the three months that they'd not been in touch. Of course, he hadn't told Cheryl of their meeting, because this would have tipped her over the edge, and besides, there was nothing to tell her, since he'd made it clear to Sandy, that his family came first, and he never wanted to see her again, apart from in passing.

Terry tried his best to distract Cheryl, for his wife was a force to be reckoned with when she was angry. She was like a psychotic patient who'd lost all touch with reality, and he feared she'd attack the woman, who would almost certainly press charges against her out of spite. So he encouraged her to keep walking.

Sandy turned around only to meet Cheryl's stare. She reacted like a rabbit caught in the headlights when she saw her with the man for whom she would have done anything in order to win his affection. But he'd disposed of her like a bag of rubbish as soon as his wife had discovered their affair. She couldn't return her stare, embarrassed at the thought of how she'd pretended to be her friend. Cheryl gave a wry smile, pleased to see her rival didn't have what it took to stand against her in a competition. Gone was the slim, toned model's body, replaced by an overweight, less-than-attractive woman. The weight she'd gained wasn't evenly distributed around her body; most of it was concentrated around her belly, giving the impression that she was at least five months pregnant, and the rest was on her face, making her look as though she had contracted the mumps. Her walk was less than graceful, and she now waddled from side to side in an attempt to carry her ton or two of lard.

Cheryl took her husband by the hand, and they headed in the same direction as the other woman. He took her hand and secured it under his, determined to show a united front. As they approached the entrance of Sainsbury's supermarket, he looked at his wife and mouthed, 'I'm so proud of you.' Many times he'd imagined them meeting Sandy, and he'd always imagined the outcome to be different from todays. He'd envisaged Cheryl having a panic attack or getting so angry that she'd rip the other woman to bits, but she'd done herself and him proud. She acted in a dignified manner. She was a class act, a true lady.

Sandy was nowhere to be seen inside the supermarket. Their guess was that she'd made her way in and then left through the exit door out, as soon as she saw that they were inside the supermarket. Nonetheless, they didn't let their guards down. Terry would stop every so often and kiss her on her cheek. When they arrived at the check-out aisle, he placed his arm around her waist and pulled her into him so that his head was resting against her shoulder. They smooched all the way back to the car park.

'She's changed drastically,' exclaimed Cheryl. 'I've never known a beauty to turn into a beast,' she said, relishing the moment. She knew only too well that her husband would never be tempted to stray into Sandy's arms again, not with her recent appearance, anyway. Terry was particular about the type of women he chose to lie with. All the women that he'd been with, as flings or in serious relationships, had one thing in common: they were all toned and slim. He had oftentimes said that fat women repulsed him, and he preferred women whom he was able to lift and carry, if need be.

Terry was careful with his response. He didn't want to ignore what Cheryl had said about the other woman, since his silence could be misconstrued as him still having an interest in her. On the other hand, giving too much negative feedback, could make him appear as though he were trying to cover up guilt.

'You'd pass her in the streets and not know it was her, if it hadn't been for her eyes,' he exclaimed. Sandy's eyes were two different colours. The right eye was piercing blue, and the left was grey. She often joked that she was the epitome of what it meant to be a combination of both her mom and dad. Her mother was a blue-eyed, blond hair Swede, and her dad had dark hair and grey eyes.

Terry now knew that his wife was on the road to recovery. She had never used the lorazepam prescribed by his friend, and she rarely touched the zopiclone. She had re-kindled her relationships with most of her friends, and would spend some of her time socialising with them. She had even seen Sandy, and that hadn't caused her to relapse. She remained a fantastic mother to their two kids, and a great wife to him. He wasn't entirely happy about her newfound social network, but being accepting of it was the least he could do to ease his guilt. But there was something that continued to be a bother to him. The bond between her and her sister Trinny was of great concern to him. He knew that Cheryl loved him and it would take an awful lot for her to leave with the kids. But if anyone could convince her to do so, it was Trinny.

Terry feared Trinny; he felt powerless over Cheryl when it came to her and her mother. For now, her mother wasn't an issue, and if she'd learnt about the problems they were having in their marriage, she didn't show it. Her behaviour toward Terry hadn't changed. He still got his invitation to join Cheryl and the kids for Sunday dinners. She was still polite and courteous to him when she visited. And she was also an old-fashioned woman with old-fashioned values. She often expressed her disapproval of divorce and believed that anyone who took such a path, was rebelling against the teachings of God.

Treasure was now approaching six, and it was both their wishes for her to attend private school. However, some of the most elite private schools were outside of their county. Once again, Terry thought that he'd use this opportunity to encourage Cheryl to agree that moving farther south in the county, would be beneficial to all, but most importantly, to the kids. Cheryl was the type of mother who would give up her own happiness if it meant that her children would be happy; she would go without (not that she ever had to) just so they could have it all, and Terry knew this only too well. Her kids were one of the reasons she chose to say in her marriage. She gave up her career just so that her marriage could work, and that was a huge sacrifice, since in doing so, she had lost a part of herself.

'Don't you think we should move closer to London, to increase the chance of Treasure and Omar getting a top-notch education?' asked Terry.

Cheryl didn't respond immediately, since she was giving herself time to think this through. The most popular elite schools that she had known were in London, and this was purely because the HRH of England had attended some of these schools. Nonetheless, they weren't cream of the crop in the field of academic achievements; on the other hand, great achievers like Terry hadn't been educated outside of Leicester, and he'd done pretty well.

'Don't you think that moving the kids to another county, where they would have no one other than you and me, will unsettle them?' she asked cautiously.

'Kids adapt quickly, and they will still be able to see their family and friends. We're not moving abroad,' he said defiantly.

'Where, exactly, do you have in mind?' she asked.

'I was thinking Hertfordshire or Bedfordshire,' he stated.

Cheryl knew that it had always been Terry's dream to live in that part of the country. Most of his university friends had resided in London and had gotten jobs in some of the most well-funded hospitals there. Most of them had gone private, since they considered working in the NHS as being beneath them. The work environment was, by far, better than Terry's. And the patients they had on their books were less violent and aggressive, although just as unwell. They joked about them having upper-class social attitude. The city workers were also based in London, as were most of the affluent rock stars, designers, and businessmen.

Cheryl tried to balance the pros and cons about moving to such a place. There were good schools in Leicester, both private and public. Her kids were proving to be great intellectuals, even at such young ages, and she had her nearest and dearest all within a two mile radius of her. She had pulled through a disastrous marriage because of the support of her sister. Trinny provided a roof for her and Treasure when her home life had become too much to bear, and she was there to stop her from falling on that night that she'd discovered Terry's transgressions. It was the thought of having her mom and Trinny so close by that aided her through her recovery from anxiety, since she knew they loved her so much that it would kill them if she had sunk any further.

She knew Terry wanted the best for his children, as much as she did, but his perception about what was best differed from hers. He was always focused on material things—he had to have the best house in the best neighbourhood, he had to drive the best car, wear the best clothing. For an intelligent man, she often wondered how he could be so shallow. For Cheryl, the best wasn't just about wealth, although not having any financial constraints did make life an awful lot easier. But she tried to balance this out with having loving, devoted people around her. She loved having her kids being able to see her parents at least three times a week, for this enabled them to develop a bond, and learn about forming relationships other than with her and Terry. She felt blessed having her sister's kids so close, since Treasure and Omar always looked forward to playing with their little cousins. They had learnt so many social skills from them, too, because they were older. This had enabled Omar and Treasure to be advanced beyond their years. And there were Terry's parents and his brothers, who were all living locally. The kids would lose out on an awful lot, she concluded to herself.

Terry impatiently sat looking at his wife. He could tell by the look on her face that she was in deep thought.

'I thought that would be an easy decision for you. What are you finding so difficult?' he asked.

'I don't think it will be in the kids' best interests to take them from everyone they know,' she retorted.

'By everyone, I take it you mean Trinny,' he said indignantly.

'Oh,' said Cheryl in exasperation. 'Now we are getting to the root of the problem. This isn't really about Treasure and Omar, is it? This is about you wanting to get rid of Trinny.'

Terry turned his head in the opposite direction of his wife's. He was livid at her behaviour, but he didn't wish to get her upset. He wanted for them to sit in a calm manner and have a peaceful discussion, because Cheryl was easier to appease when she deemed others to be working with her, as opposed to against her. He knew if he angered her, she would stick her heels in and refuse to accept any suggestion he'd make.

They sat quietly for a while. He was suddenly engrossed by the news on the television, while she sat fuming about his earlier statement.

'Oh look!' he said with astonishment. 'That's one of the victims that I performed surgery on during the explosion in London!'

A documentary highlighting the tragedy that took place on that dreadful day not too long ago was on the television. Many lives—and limbs too—were lost. Terry was one of the operating doctors who used his much-needed skills on that day to save many lives. He remembered this particular woman, because not only did he have to amputate her leg above the knee to save her from dying, but he also had to break the news to her about her husband's passing away.

* * *

The couple had been caught up in the carnage; her leg had been blown to pieces, and she was losing blood rapidly. Her leg, from her knee down, had turned black because it had lost its life due to the lack of oxygenated blood reaching it. She had many more injuries, but that was, by far, the worst. Terry and his team had spent eleven hours in theatre trying to save what they could of her leg, as well as trying to save her life. He'd spent such a long time with her in theatre, that he felt he had grown to know her.

It was seven days later, after they'd manage to stabilise her, that Terry was asked by one of his colleagues to break the news to her. The woman's husband had been brought into theatre with his guts hanging out; collateral from the explosion had ripped right through him. The paramedics had fought tirelessly to save his life, but he had lost so much blood by the time they had arrived, that he died shortly after arriving at the hospital.

Terry had performed many surgeries since qualifying as a surgeon, but none of his patients' plights had ever moved him as this woman's had. She had suffered two great losses that could never be replaced, for not only had she lost her leg, but she'd lost her husband too. The one person whom she was probably relying on to help her through this darkness was taken away from her by some callous, satanic brutes. *How could anyone retain their sanity after such a loss?* he'd thought to himself back then.

As Terry approached her bay, she looked up at him and gave a smile. The truth was, she viewed him in the same way that she viewed God. God created her life, and this doctor had saved her life. Without him and his expertise, she knew she would have died.

'My husband?' she muttered to one of the nurses who had come to change her wet bed linen. 'Where's my husband?' It was the first time since she was brought into hospital, that she'd asked for her husband. The doctors suspected that she had suffered temporary memory loss.

The covering doctor was informed of her enquiry, and he'd made a phone call to Terry, asking that he do him a favour. He thought the woman would be able to take some solace from being told about the loss of her husband by Terry.

She'd grabbed hold of his shirt on hearing the news and let out a cry that lingered in Terry's ears for months to come. He was a surgeon who'd found himself being a counsellor and comforter. He'd gone beyond and above his call of duty. His years at university, and as a junior doctor, had helped to prepare him for coping with horrendous injuries and the people who lost a leg or two, but it had never prepared him for dealing with anyone who'd encountered such a loss. The memories of this woman had never left his mind. Her screams occasionally echoed in his ears.

* * *

Cheryl sat up straight to view the woman and listen to her account of that dreadful day. She could see how touched her husband was by this woman's appearance. He had gone through so much on his own because she was too unwell at the time to give him any support. A tear ran down Terry's face as the woman praised the medical team that was involved in her care on that day and many days after. Cheryl was consumed with guilt at seeing his reaction, for her reaction on that day, when he arrived home, was still fresh in her thoughts. She knelt in front of her husband and took his face in her hands and gently kissed him on the forehead.

'I'm so sorry I wasn't there for you,' she said compassionately.

He kissed her on the nose and let his finger glide across her lips.

'You were too sick to grasp ...' He stopped himself before he could finish his sentence, for he was once again reminded of how much hurt he'd caused his wife. Her anxiety was evident. He took her in his hands and held her so tightly that she felt like her breath was leaving her body. 'I'm so sorry,' he said. 'I promise, I'll never hurt you like that again.'

Cheryl knew that he meant every word that he'd just uttered to her and felt a sense of relief and comfort from it.

'We'll be okay, won't we?' she asked.

'We'll be more than okay, darling. We'll be fine, we'll be fine.'

They sat down to watch the rest of the documentary, with Terry filling Cheryl in on all that he had gone through that day. It had been four years since the disaster had struck in London, and he was affected by it in more ways than one. But he'd never been able to disclose to or discuss with his wife what he had encountered due to her ill health, and now he could. He saw this as another confirmation that she had truly recovered from her anxiety.

* * *

The issue about moving to the south of the country was still preying on Terry's mind. He was hesitant to raise the topic because it had been met with such a frosty reception previously, and he also knew that it would be upsetting for Cheryl if she had to move away from her family. He didn't wish to cause her any more pain than he had already done. He was terrified at the prospect of losing his wife, and he felt that living so close to Trinny, with Cheryl being able to see her on a regular basis, could result in the destruction of his marriage. The two women had always been close, but they had formed a deeper and special bond when Cheryl took ill.

Cheryl and Trinny had arranged a day out with the kids after her return from the Caribbean, and when Cheryl told Terry about their plans, he became as white as sheet. It was as though all the blood had drained from his body.

'Where are you taking them?' he asked anxiously.

'Lego Land,' replied Cheryl.

'Don't you think that the kids are too young for such an adventure?' he asked with concern.

Cheryl wasn't convinced, especially since they had taken the kids to Disneyland in Paris the previous year. They were a year younger then, and as far as Cheryl was concerned, Disneyland was a far more daunting theme park than Lego Land.

On their day at Lego Land, Cheryl had never seen Treasure and Omar have so much fun. They were happy at the prospect of being at Lego Land, but they were even more elated that they had their three cousins to share the fun with. They ate ice cream, rode on most of the rides, and took part in the activities taking place that day. But whilst the rest of the family were having fun, Terry clearly wasn't. He rang Cheryl more than ten times within five hours, pretending that he wanted to find out about the kids' progress and declaring his undying love for her. But he was clearly anxious about the discussion that the two women were having amongst themselves. He had thoughts of Trinny convincing his wife to take their kids and leave him, and he feared that, left alone with Trinny, Cheryl might just succumb to her influence.

Terry returned home from work that evening earlier than he normally did. He had taken emergency annual leave because he was unable to commit himself to his job; his mind was occupied by the two women. The hospital had had to postpone a surgery that was scheduled for later that evening, because Terry was scheduled to be the operating doctor, and it was difficult to find a replacement surgeon at such short notice.

Cheryl was taken aback to find her husband at home so early. He looked pale in colour, and his usual smiley face was replaced by a sullen-looking one. Her heart skipped a beat when she approached him.

'What's wrong?' she asked, concerned.

'Why?' responded Terry.

'You're never home this early', she exclaimed.

'Is it wrong for a man to want to spend some quality time with his wife?' said Terry as he pulled her closer to him.

Cheryl took a deep breath before letting it all out in one big sigh. It was as if a huge weight had been lifted off her shoulders.

He ripped her blouse open, sending the buttons flying in various directions across the room. He cupped her breasts in his hands before unsnapping her bra, allowing himself to take in the full view of her breasts as they fell free from her bra. With his breathing becoming heavier and louder, he buried his face between her breasts whilst feeling for the crotch of her knickers. With his bare hands, he ripped both side of her knickers and parted her legs.

Cheryl screamed out amidst the pleasure of her husband entering her, and he was like a wild animal that had just been let out of its cage. He was rough, yet passionate, and she could feel her body begging for more of him. His hot breath, breathing on her neck, stimulated her even more. His deep and fast thrust was so sensual. Her legs became numb beneath her. She lost herself somewhere in between the onset of her orgasm and the peak of it. She was unable to recollect what happened thereabouts, since she had been totally oblivious to everything. She came out of her pleasurable state to find her husband lying on top of her, with his body going through spasms. It was all so surreal; it was like she'd died and gone to heaven.

* * *

As they viewed the prospectuses sent to them by various private schools, both in Leicester and London, Terry did his best to paint the local schools in a negative manner. He was critical of their Ofsted report and was less than pleased about the percentage of kids absent on a regular basis.

'This is mediocre,' he fumed. 'The public schools in Hertfordshire perform at a higher standard than these so-called private schools,' he said indignantly. Cheryl could see his point about the percentage of kids who were absent on a regular basis, because most of the schools they had viewed locally, had a consistent absentee rate of 5.9 percent, way above that of their counterparts in Hertfordshire. She looked at her husband in dismay, she was now confused. She didn't want to be responsible for her kids not getting a good education, but she also didn't want to take them from everyone and everything they had grown to know and become fond of over the years.

Chapter 27

It had been six months since Terry and his family had moved to Hertfordshire. The neighbourhood was clearly an affluent one, boasting palatial mansions with wide, sweeping gardens. Every one of their neighbours seemed to be a proud owner of a Jaguar, Mercedes, or BMW. Terry fit in quite well, and at least two of his long-time friends lived on the neighbouring streets. He had gotten a job as the senior surgeon at a popular hospital in London. Life was fantastic for him, since he had achieved his goal. Terry had always wanted to live in Hertfordshire after he'd finished his training, but was prevented by Cheryl, who didn't wish to live away from her family.

Terry had seen this as a hindrance, and whilst he did his best to not let Cheryl knew how much he resented her from reaching his goal, he had been seething inside. He frowned up on their neighbours in Leicester as 'common muck,' for they weren't as affluent as those in the crowd who populated his tight social circle. Sure, they drove expensive cars and their homes were rather nice too, but all these were middle-class achievements to Terry, and he'd always thought that he could do far better.

The kids had started school; they were both enrolled at the Bishop's Stratford Junior School. Their academic achievement was superb, and their absentee record, well, it wasn't perfect, but it was better than those at the local schools they had viewed in Leicester. It was comforting for Cheryl to know that Treasure and Omar were both attending the same school, because it meant that they had each other. They had become disgruntled little kids, and they quite frequently voiced how unhappy they were about not being able to see Nana Sue, Nana Gladys, Aunty Trinny, and their little cousins. This broke Cheryl's heart. She hadn't settled in because she was some hundred or more miles away from her family and friends. But at least if her kids had been happy, she would have been able to sacrifice her happiness for them.

Cheryl hadn't managed to form any close bonds with the other moms at her children's school. She had found the other women to be pompous and rude, or so dumb that they were unable to string two words together, let alone a sentence. Terry's friends were single men, one of whom still lived at home with his parents.

With no meaningful activities to do, no close friends to visit, and the kids being away at school for at least six hours a day, Cheryl started to show a relapse in her mental health. Terry had started to spend some of his weekends away with his single friends, leaving her feeling neglected and abandoned. She hadn't been sleeping properly, and found that she needed the help of her zopiclone to aid her. She became quite anxious too, especially when Terry was away with his single friends. The memories of the Sandy incident came flooding back.

And Cheryl found herself clutching the kids close to her whilst stooping in a foetal like position, guarding them with her body.

'Hi, Cheryl. It's your mom,' said the voice on the other end of the phone. 'I haven't heard from you for the past week, and I'm getting a bit concerned, darling; please give me a ring.'

The kids looked at their mom, perplexed. Their mom and Grandma used to call each other every day, and would spend hours on the phone, and they had been able to speak to their grandmother. But now, all communication had stopped. It had been two weeks since they last spoke to their grandma and aunties and uncles. They hadn't been to school for the past four days because their mom had told them that someone was out to get them.

Cheryl was behaving strangely. She wouldn't let the children out of her sight. If she was going to the toilet, they had to go with her; they all had their baths together. And they all had to constantly wear the colour red, because Cheryl had told them that it gave them protection from the force that was after them. They weren't able to watch television; Cheryl told them that the television was telling her to do evil things. Treasure sensed that there was something terribly wrong with her mother, but she was terrified at disclosing any details about her mother's behaviour to anyone, out of fear that she and her brother might be taken away from their mother.

Their mother had been acting strange, but she was the best mother in the entire universe, as far as they were concerned. She cooked them delicious meals, bathed them in their favourite scented bath oil, gave them the best gifts and lots of cuddles, and read them a story each at night.

Treasure was now ten years old and continued to be advanced for a child her age. She knew what mental illness was because her mom had told her stories about the patients whom she had come in contact with when she was a pharmacist.

She looked her mother in the eye, and with her voice just more than a whisper, she said. 'Mommy, are you now unwell, like one of your former patients?'

'Why?' asked Cheryl, curious. 'I'm only trying to protect you and your brother. The evil forces are out to get us.'

Terry returned home from work earlier than expected that afternoon to find Treasure and Omar at home, sitting on their mom's knee. The drapes were drawn, the bulbs had been taken out of their sockets, and the television was off. The house was dark and hot, as if the heating had been on for a whole month continuously. . He looked at his family with incredulity.

'Why aren't the kids in school?' he asked with surprised.

Cheryl didn't respond. She just stared at him, as if she were looking through him. She pulled her kids close to her, and held them so tight that little Omar was unable to breathe.

'You're hurting me, Mommy!' he exclaimed.

Terry stepped forward to release the kids from her grip. Cheryl tightened her grip and started to chant, barely understandable. Terry held his head in his hands; he was astonished by his wife's behaviour. He'd noticed that she had changed since their move from Leicester, but he'd put her behaviour down to the fact that she had moved away from her family and friends. He'd told himself that she'd return to her former self once she had settled in.

Where was I when this was happening? he asked himself. His wife had now gone psychotic, and he hadn't noticed. He got on the phone and called his mother and brothers, after which he called Cheryl's mom. He knew that he now needed all the help of those who are close to her. He couldn't pretend that this wasn't happening anymore. He knew the score; he knew what needed to be done.

Cheryl was admitted to the priory under a section two of the mental health act. She was diagnosed with psychotic depression combined with anxiety. Treating her wasn't easy because she had knowledge about every drug and its side effects.

'I won't take that; it will give me amnesia, and I most definitely won't be taking that,' she informed the consultant who had just prescribed a high dosage of Citalopram, twenty milligrams once daily, and Risperidone, one milligram.

'I'll take Sertraline, fifty milligrams. You've diagnosed me with psychotic depression. For goodness sake, treat me so that I can go home to my kids and still be of use to them. If you treatment my depression, you'll find that my psychosis will eventually go; my psychosis is secondary to my depression,' she proclaimed.

Terry looked on, pleased, because he recognised that his wife had now acknowledged that she was unwell. She had initially refused treatment and had to be coerced to get it after she was informed that her section two would be regraded as a section three so that they could enforce treatment. Although she was a difficult patient, challenging the nurses and doctors about their plan of treatment for her, she was never abusive, and the decisions that she made about her plan of care had all been effective for her.

Two weeks later, Cheryl was back in Leicester with her family. Terry had seen first-hand how detrimental it was to her mental health, to take her away from her friends and family. When they had moved to Hertfordshire, they hadn't put their home up for sale because they had decided to give themselves a trial period before selling it permanently. It had proven wise to do so, and the family was able to return home without the additional stress of having to look for suitable accommodations.

Cheryl was back in the same county as her family and most of her friends. And although she didn't have any employment, she had meaningful activities. She would go shopping with her friends, and she would visit her mom on a regular basis. She'd often sit and watch her kids play with their cousins, whilst she and Trinny helped their mom cook a big family feast. This, to her, was meaningful, as she looked around and saw that all the people whom she loved were within a close proximity of her. She knew she had done the right thing by agreeing to return home.

She hoped that one day her sister would accept her reasons for staying in her marriage. When Cheryl took her vow 'until death do we part,' she meant it literally.

Lightning Source UK Ltd.
Milton Keynes UK
UKOW052204041111

181507UK00001B/22/P